A TRUE BLUE KNIGHT

BY

ROSEANNE WILLIAMS

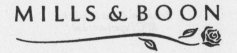

MILLS & BOON

*MILLS & BOON and the Rose Device are trademarks of the publisher.
TEMPTATION is a trademark of Harlequin Enterprises Limited, used
under licence.
This edition published by arrangement with Harlequin Enterprises B.V.
First published in Great Britain in 1995
by Harlequin Mills & Boon Limited, Eton House, 18-24 Paradise Road,
Richmond, Surrey TW9 1SR*

© Sheila Slattery 1994

ISBN 0 263 79287 0

21 - 9505

*Printed in Great Britain by
BPC Paperbacks Ltd*

"Is it warm in here, or is it me?"

Tomasina had become aware of a sudden rise in the room temperature.

"It's us," Brogue murmured, stepping closer to her. "Body heat." He lifted his finger to her chin and tipped her face up to his.

Tomasina looked up at him. "Brogue, something strange is happening in this house. I can't explain it, but—"

"I can," he assured her. "It's irresistible attraction."

"Brogue, I'm getting scared."

Her lip trembled and he stilled it with his thumb. "Listen, Tomasina, I'm a cop, remember? You're safe."

"Don't you feel something wrong in here?"

Brogue drew her into his arms. "All I feel is you. All I *want* to feel is you."

ROSEANNE WILLIAMS
is also the author
of these novels in
Temptation

THE MAGIC TOUCH
LOVE CONQUERS ALL
UNDER THE COVERS
THE BAD BOY
MAIL ORDER MAN
SEEING RED

Prologue

KATHRYN POWELL BREATHED her last on New Year's Day in her butterfly garden at the ripe age of eighty-four. The end came for her in the most peaceful, painless way she could ever have imagined—and Kat had *quite* an imagination.

In the hereafter, Kat was reunited with loved ones who had made the transition before her. Her brother, Derek, and her next-door neighbor Samantha had always been especially dear to her.

During their lives on Earth, Derek and Samantha had been an odd match: Samantha an anxious, ladylike, spinster schoolteacher; Derek a strapping, soldier of fortune—and a married man to boot. Kat, a spinster herself, had always understood and supported their love for each other.

Soon after the reunion, Kat was advised that she could remain eternally in the everafter. Unless, that is, she first wished to tie up any loose ends she'd left in her previous reality. If so, she could opt to be a ghost for a while. A good ghost, of course, with an unselfish purpose.

"Yes," Kat decided, after giving the option careful thought. "I never wrote out a will that would leave my butterfly garden to those who I know would cherish and preserve it. My death came too suddenly...so now I must return and ensure the garden's future. Not that I know the first thing about being a ghost."

Knowing no more than Kat did about it, Derek and Samantha offered to go along with her and help. Besides, they, too, had left loose ends behind.

"What an irony for me to be a ghost," Kat marveled. "Before I died, I always thought I had a ghost in my house, but now I see it was only a figment of my high-flying imagination."

"I always admired your imagination," Samantha said with a nostalgic smile. "You were always so positive and playful, the exact opposite of me, the worrywart."

Kat chuckled merrily. "That ghost was one of my best mental creations. Osgood."

Laughing with Kat, Sam said, "No one could talk you out of believing that Osgood was haunting your house. I worried endlessly about whether you'd gone off the deep end."

"You worried about *everything*, not just Osgood," Kat recalled. "Opposites that you and I were—your glass always half empty and mine always half full—it's a wonder we became best friends."

Derek shook his head. "No wonder that, since opposites attract. If they didn't," he said, gazing at Samantha, "my dearest Sam and I wouldn't have fallen in love with each other."

Sam cuddled up to him and stroked his cheek. "Thank heaven our love is no longer forbidden. True love is as it should be here—free of legalities and boundaries."

"Hear, hear," Kat agreed. "But after all the two of you have been through together on Earth, are you sure you want to return with me as ghosts?"

Derek nodded. "There's something I must do there. I earned a pocketful of diamonds back when I was hired on to guard a diamond mine in Brazil. My distrust of banks kept me from selling the jewels and putting the cash into an account. Instead, I kept them hidden in a secret place."

Kat was surprised by his words. "Why, I always thought you were telling tall tales about the mine. You did have a habit of embellishing the facts when you told stories of your adventures."

He grinned. "A few of my tales were true in every amazing detail, sis. I buried the diamonds to save for my old age, then died from a stroke before I needed them. Now I'd like someone to benefit from my treasure."

"And I also have something I left undone," Samantha said. "I taught many lessons when I was a schoolteacher, but never did convince my niece, Tomasina, that true love is worth any cost. I must go back and make certain she learns the most important lesson of all."

And so Kat, Derek and Sam—with permission from the highest authority—became ghosts and returned to San Francisco, California. They established residence in the Victorian house where Kat had lived for fifty years and started helping each other tie up their loose ends....

1

TOMASINA WALDEN WOULD never have become a
Peeping Tom if the house next door hadn't gone up for
sale. When it did, she quickly became an expert at using a knothole in her back fence to peek into the neighboring yard.

Yes, a disgusting way for a respectable, twenty-eight-
year-old schoolteacher to react whenever she noticed
the house being shown to a prospective buyer. But she
had reasons to peek at anyone who wanted to see that
house, reasons to eavesdrop on whatever was said
when they came out to look at the big, rambling garden behind it. Good reasons.

This morning—a windy Friday in March—an agent
was showing someone through, so Tomasina was at the
knothole, waiting for them to come out the back door.
She gathered her long blond hair in one hand so it
wouldn't fly up in the wind and show over the top of
the fence.

Shivering, she wished that she'd put on a sweater
before she had hurried outside dressed in a hot-pink
leotard and neon-yellow tights. She'd been all set to do
video aerobics, when she'd glanced through the window and seen a car parked next door, a sign that the
house was being shown.

It was a Victorian, like her own home, one of San Francisco's "painted ladies," so called for their colorful paint work. She had been close friends with the elderly owner, Kathryn Powell, who had died in January. They had spent countless happy hours together tending Kat's backyard garden. It was sad now to think of Kat, who had died of a stroke there one day when they were gardening together.

Tomasina noticed the back door of the house open. She glued her eye to the knothole and instantly recognized the tall, dark-haired, drop-dead gorgeous man who came out on the back step. Brogue Donovan! He was the cop who'd given a crime-prevention talk at the elementary school where she taught third grade.

Tomasina shivered again—but not because of the cold—as she took in Lieutenant Donovan's silver-blue eyes and muscular build. She couldn't deny that he'd been a heartthrob in his police uniform at the school two weeks ago, a true blue knight. Out of uniform—in jeans, a knit shirt and a leather bomber jacket—he was no less of a hunk.

Breathless, Tomasina watched him frown as he surveyed the tangled undergrowth beneath the blooming goose-plum and cherry trees that Kat had planted fifty years earlier.

Another man, short and gray haired, came out of the house and joined him on the step. A real estate agent, Tomasina surmised. She was dying to hear what they'd say.

"Talk about urban jungles," Brogue said.

It's heaven on Earth to city butterflies, Tomasina wanted to retort.

Brogue spoke again, with apparent disgust. "What a mess of weeds and mud puddles."

The agent said, "According to the fact sheet, this is a rare, old-fashioned butterfly garden."

Brogue snorted derisively.

Tomasina couldn't help but feel insulted. She and Kat had worked hard to plant and nurture every mundane, messy weed necessary to butterfly survival: nettles, thistles, milkweed, mustard, wild anise, Bermuda grass, and more.

Brogue's look of disgust smoothed into a smile that Tomasina found heart-stoppingly attractive, even though she never let herself get attracted to cops.

Brogue smiled wider and said, "This yard is just the right size, though."

The right size for what? Tomasina fearfully wondered.

The garden was a constant worry, since Kat hadn't left a will and didn't have any living relatives to inherit the property. An expert on butterflies, Kat had always said she wished to leave everything to the Flying Flowers Society, a group dedicated to protecting urban butterfly habitats. But without a will, ownership had gone to the state of California, which had put the property up for sale.

Tomasina couldn't sell her own Victorian to buy the other—not even for a good cause—because her house had been in the Walden family since 1878. It was an heirloom, priceless in sentiment and family history.

"Matter of fact, this yard is perfect," Brogue said, sounding increasingly pleased.

Tomasina chewed her lower lip. *Perfect for what?*

The agent said, "The price is right, too."

Tomasina anxiously bit off her thumbnail. She thought of how hard the society was working to raise funds to buy the house and preserve the garden. Only a small fraction of the price had been raised so far.

With the garden in jeopardy now, hundreds of butterflies were in danger. In fact, they were metamorphosing in Tomasina's own kitchen at this very moment! Two hundred good reasons for her to care what happened to Kat's garden.

Her heart stopped as Brogue turned suddenly and stared straight at the section of high pine fence that hid her from him. She recoiled from his penetrating gaze, even though she knew he couldn't see her spying through the deep-set hole.

He stared for only two seconds, but it seemed like forever to Tomasina before he looked away. She went limp with relief and refocused on the two men as they came down the steps and stood looking out on the garden.

"This is the biggest backyard in this part of town," the agent advised. "The other lots are postage stamps compared with this."

"Perfect," Brogue said again. "I'll put a covered swimming pool on the left half and a sports court on the right half."

Tomasina clapped her hand over her mouth and smothered a groan of dismay. She said a quick, silent prayer to Mother Nature, *Don't let him buy it. Please keep it for sale until the society raises enough money.*

Then she jerked back again as Brogue's riveting eyes returned to the fence. She *knew* he couldn't see her spying through the hole; she'd already checked it out from the other side. Heaven help her if he was one of those cops who had a sixth sense about being watched. The way he kept staring in her direction was uncanny.

"What do you know about the neighbors on either side?" Brogue asked, turning back to the agent.

The agent flipped through a notepad. "Let's see . . . I did some research . . . there's a retired couple on the left and a schoolteacher on the right. She got an okay from the state to maintain the yard and keep an eye on the house while it's on the market."

"She's done a dirt-poor job on the yard so far," Brogue observed, raising his voice. "I hope the neighbors on both sides mind their own business and keep to themselves."

Ordinarily, I would, Tomasina mentally huffed. *Only for the garden's sake am I spying like this.*

"If there's anything I can't stand," Brogue went on, staring in the direction of the fence again, "it's nosy neighbors. Noisy ones, too."

Tomasina had an immediate urge to run inside and turn on her stereo full blast. But she didn't want to miss a word of what they said.

"I've never heard any complaints of that kind about this neighborhood," the agent said reassuringly. "You could easily check it out on your police computer to make sure."

"I already have," Brogue replied. "This is a low-crime, low-profile area. No peace disturbances. I didn't have time to check out the next-door neighbors, though. Thanks for thinking of it."

"So," said the agent to Brogue, "what do you say?"

"I want to make a formal offer," Brogue replied. "Let's go hash out the details and write things up."

Tomasina couldn't let him do that. She had to stop him, but how? He and the agent were turning to leave. There must be something she could do that would change his mind about buying the house. He'd said he hated nosy neighbors. Noisy ones, too. She'd better be both. Right now!

"Oh, yoo-hoo," she called out. "Who's that I see through the peephole in my fence?"

She released her hair, letting the wind carry the long strands up and show the two men exactly where she was. Then she hooked her fingers on the top of the fence and pulled herself up to peer over at them.

"Hi, there. Oh, what a beautiful March morning, isn't it? If you'd like to know about everything wrong with that house before you buy, I can tell you."

She was gratified to see the agent look severely pained. It was just as pleasing to see Brogue's dark eyebrows rise with obvious concern and curiosity.

"Wrong?" Brogue questioned.

"Thanks, ma'am," the agent sputtered, "but we don't need any—"

"Oh, I'd just *love* to fill you in on what's wrong with it," she chirped, doing her utmost to sound like a bustling snoop, an interfering busybody, a nosy neighbor straight from hell. "I know every small—and not so small—problem it has. Just stay right where you are while I pop through the driveway gate."

The agent protested, "Ma'am, we really don't—"

"Stay put. Here I come." Tomasina sped to the gate, barged into Kat's backyard and introduced herself to the dismayed agent first.

"I'm Miss Tomasina Walden," she said, forcing an energetic, excessively enthusiastic handshake on him. "Yes, Walden as in Walden Pond, and *Miss* instead of Mrs. because I've had the worst luck you can imagine with men who aren't good listeners. Naturally, because of my last name, my all-time favorite author is Henry David Thoreau, who wrote *Walden Pond*," she babbled off the top of her head.

She formed a circle with her thumb and forefinger and coyly held it up to one eye. "I guess you could also call me Peeping Tom, couldn't you? That knothole is just the right height for me to see everything over here. And your name, sir, is . . . ?"

"Grant," the agent muttered. "Harvey Grant." He gave Brogue a sinking look. "This is my client, Bro—"

"Of course! Lieutenant Brogue Donovan, S.F.P.D.," she gushed, seizing Brogue's hand and working it up and down like the lever of a tire jack. "You spoke to the children at my school not long ago—Serra Vista Elementary, where I've been a teacher ever since I graduated from the teaching program at the University of Southern California five years ago."

She blabbered, "Serra Vista is the largest elementary school in the city, with hundreds of kids and half as many teachers, so you probably don't remember me. But we all remember *you* teaching us how to avoid crime."

She finally ran out of breath, giving Brogue a chance to speak.

"I remember you that day, Miss Walden. You wore a blue sweatery dress and a butterfly pin."

Tomasina stopped herself from feeling flattered. She told herself, as she always did, that most men noticed blond, bosomy women. There were pluses and minuses to being noticeable in that way, enough of both to keep her levelheaded about the knee-jerk response her features usually got from the opposite sex.

"You must have a photographic memory," she said, attempting to downplay Brogue's compliment and continue being a chatterbox at the same time.

He spoke again before she could gain momentum. "Is this a school holiday, or do you always get Mondays off?"

"I'm job-sharing this semester in order to do some postgrad study at SFSU," she replied. "Tuesday and Thursday are my workdays this week. But let me tell you about Kat Powell. She was the dearest neighbor in the world and I'm sure she'd want you to know about the butterfly garden she loved more than anything else.

"Naturally, I eavesdropped on every word you said about clearing it out and putting in a covered swimming pool and a sports court. Which I'm sure you were just kidding about, weren't you?"

"No kidding," Brogue said, surprised that she was soliciting a reply.

"No?" She didn't have to pretend to appear as devastated as she felt. "Kat would be heartbroken to see her beloved garden all torn out. Surely you wouldn't want to break her heart. Would you? I mean—"

Harvey cleared his throat and interrupted, "Since she isn't alive now, she won't 'see' anything."

"Well, of course not," Tomasina allowed. "Not literally. But I'm certain she'll sense it just the same. She was very sensitive, you see, and committed her life to this garden. It—"

"Committed to weeds?" Brogue cut in, surveying the yard dubiously.

"Weeds are plants that city butterflies need in order to survive," Tomasina earnestly informed him, hopeful that a basic education on environmental necessities would be all he'd need to see what he was missing. "If you clear out the garden, you'll be clearing out the endangered butterflies, too."

"So?" Brogue shrugged. "They've got Golden Gate Park to live in. Besides, I'm the farthest thing you'll ever find from a nature freak. You aren't one, are you?"

Tomasina decided she'd better not reveal her active membership in the Flying Flowers Society. She didn't want him knowing she had her own personal reasons to discourage him from buying the house.

"Kat loved nature," she replied, evading his question. Seeing no hope of kindling a kindred spirit in him, she switched tactics, from environmental to spiritual. "Butterflies were symbols of hope and inspiration to Kat, sort of like—" She stopped short, trying to think up a long-winded comparison.

"Like chasing rainbows?" Brogue sardonically suggested, one eyebrow arching cynically.

From that and his unsympathetic replies so far, Tomasina got the message that Brogue was one of those city-gritty, tough-as-nails cops who wouldn't be caught dead getting inspired by anything.

She'd have to go for broke now and paint a dark, rundown picture of the house he thought he wanted to buy.

"Aside from Kat's avid interest in the plants she grew, I'm sure she'd want you to know about the roof problem this house has. It—"

"Roof problem?" Harvey repeated, looking severely pained again.

"Mmm-hmm. The leaks." Tomasina could only think of two tiny ones, but two were enough to form a plural. Enough to make any hard-core realist think drip, drip. Enough to inspire nightmares about dry rot and mildew.

Brogue frowned up at the roof. "Sure hope it can be patched."

Tomasina gave it a hopeless glance. "Kat would want you to know about the water pipes, too, and the—"

"Pipes?" Harvey croaked, his eyes beginning to glaze.

"They groan," Tomasina gravely advised. Only two seldom-used water lines actually did that, but they groaned nonetheless. Discouraging to any potential buyer, to say the least.

Brogue asked, "What else is wrong with this place?"

"Besides the roof and the pipes," Tomasina obligingly continued, "there's the ghost."

Harvey's glazed eyes rolled shut and his lips formed the G word without any sound.

"Come on, Miss Walden," Brogue said. "Ghost? There's no such thing."

"According to Kat there's one in permanent residence here," she truthfully affirmed, for Kat had often claimed that the house was haunted by a ghost. "Kat described it as a disembodied spirit who walked through walls and made icy cold spots in the air."

Tomasina conveniently neglected to add that Kat had been an imaginative eccentric who'd been avidly interested in UFOs, Bigfoot and Tessie, the Lake Tahoe monster.

Brogue scoffed, "I don't believe in ghosts. You aren't saying you've seen any, are you?"

"Oh, no," Tomasina replied, "but Kat always insisted she'd seen something ghostly many times in the past few years."

Brogue shook his head dismissively. "No such thing as ghosts. No way."

Without agreeing or disagreeing, Tomasina said, "Either way, aren't you glad to find out beforehand, so you'll know what it is if you see it walking through the walls? Kat kept the phone number of an exorcist handy, even though she never got haunted to the point of calling him. She—"

Brogue cut her short. "How long have you lived next door?"

"Almost as long as I've been a teacher. You see, I inherited my house from my aunt Samantha, since I was her only niece and she doted on me to the point that she willed me everything she owned before she passed away five years ago."

It was a marathon effort for Tomasina to keep chattering like this, but she gave it her all for Kat.

"Aunt Sam was a spinster schoolteacher—as I am—who lived alone—as I do—with nothing to pay attention to but her neighbors after she retired. She was the world's biggest, most lovable worrywart and everybody on the block called her Good Neighbor Sam."

Tomasina stopped, hearing a rustling sound come from a patch of tall grass under the nearest goose-plum tree. Then she almost jumped for joy as a small, furry, black-and-white creature peeked out through the grass stems at her.

"Oh, no!" she exclaimed, pointing it out to Brogue and Harvey. "A skunk!"

Harvey's mouth dropped open. Brogue's jaw clenched.

Tomasina didn't give any indication that the skunk was as tame as a house cat. She didn't call out his name—Airwick—or divulge that he didn't have scent glands. She didn't breathe a word about how he had appeared in the garden one day, become close friends with Kat and lived there as a pet ever since.

She just pinched her nostrils shut and kept talking. "Skunks are a highly protected species of urban wildlife. Killing or trapping them is illegal, so the best you can do is keep your distance when one lives in your backyard."

Harvey covered his nose with one hand and backed up quickly toward the steps. "We've got to go, ma'am."

"Right now? Stay a minute more and I'll show you where Osgood Everett Powell died a long, lingering death upstairs in Kat's house."

This was the honest-to-goodness truth, since naming houseplants had been one of Kat's harmless, charming fancies. Osgood had been a spindly, stunted, sickly fern.

"Kat nursed his chronic illness for years," Tomasina babbled, dogging the two men to the door, "and the day after he died, his ghost started haunting the house. Or so Kat believed. She and Osgood were—"

"Some other time, Miss Walden," Brogue said. He went up the steps, three at a time. "We're late. For something."

"If you'd like a Girl Scout cookie and a neighborly cup of tea before you go, I can brew up a fresh pot in no time at all," she trilled as Brogue and Harvey escaped into the house through the back door.

Less than a minute later, she heard the car start up and drive away. Kneeling, she beckoned to Airwick, who trotted out of the weeds and let her scratch his head. "Thanks for showing up when you did," she murmured. "I was running out of hot air."

Airwick burrowed his nose into her palm, then looked up into her eyes and made a mournful little skunk sound.

"I know how much you miss Kat," Tomasina sympathized. "I miss her, too."

She took comfort in petting him for a few minutes, then watched him wander back into the garden.

So much for Brogue's offer, she exulted to herself. Too bad for him that he'd wanted to destroy Kat's garden. And too bad that he wasn't a nature lover who would have responded to all the good reasons that the garden should stay.

And too bad he was a cop, which was all the more reason to discourage him from being her next-door neighbor. She never dated cops or even got friendly with them. Never, no matter what.

Her father had been one of L.A.P.D.'s finest sergeants, shot dead in the line of duty. Her sister had followed in his footsteps and met the same tragic fate in her rookie year. So it would take more than hell freezing over for Tomasina to let a cop come into her life. Having two in the family had cost too much.

Having one next door—who hadn't forgotten her dress, her butterfly pin and heaven knows what else—would have been one too many.

Still, as relieved as she felt about saving the garden from him, she couldn't help regretting that Brogue Donovan had three big strikes against him.

Tomasina sighed, recalling his talk at the school and how he'd gained an instant rapport with the kids, how he'd gotten his crime prevention message across with ease and gruff humor. He'd struck just the right note. Every female teacher had been hyperventilating about him since then, and the school nurse had even taken it upon herself to find out that he was divorced, without children and unattached.

Tomasina thought of Brogue's sexy, if hard-edged, smile. She recalled his husky voice, his riveting eyes, his muscular, masculine build. If only he'd been a nature lover, and not a cop, she would have put out the welcome mat and invited him to borrow a cup of sugar...anytime...day or night....

Too bad.

2

KAT, DEREK AND SAMANTHA met by the goose-plum tree after everyone had left the garden.

The three of them—although invisible to everyone else—were visible to each other and had taken on the physical appearances from their former lives.

Kat was plump and grandmotherly, comfortable in a muslin gardening smock, Dutch clogs and a floppy-brimmed straw hat. Derek, burly and bearded, was often outfitted for action and adventure in jungle fatigues and seven-league boots. Samantha, wispy and delicate, wore a lace-collared pastel frock and kept a long string of worry beads slipping through her nervous fingers.

"Matchmaking wasn't part of my original plan," Sam said with an anxious flutter in her voice. "I wonder if I should try it now that Brogue has unexpectedly appeared on the scene. He and Tomasina may be good for each other, or maybe not. It's so hard to tell."

She looked for confirmation from Kat, who said, "Despite his blind spot when it comes to butterflies, Brogue seems like a good match for Tomasina. Precisely what she needs to learn her lesson." Kat let out a chuckle. "She was quite inventive about running him away, wasn't she?"

Derek corrected her. "*You* ran Brogue away when you woke up Airwick and got him to come out of his burrow."

"I do have a garden to save," Kat said, defending herself. "Airwick is a natural deterrent, so what else could I do but call him out?"

Derek replied, "Before Airwick appeared, Brogue couldn't keep his eyes off Tomasina."

Kat gazed down at the garden. "Imagine Brogue wanting to mow down my greatest pride and joy. Tsk, tsk. He has so much to learn about Mother Nature."

"If he ever comes back," Samantha said, fretting, owl eyed with anxiety. "What if he doesn't?"

Derek maintained with swashbuckling certainty, "He will. It's going to take more than Airwick to keep a man's man away from Tomasina. It takes one to know one, you know."

DRIVING BACK to the realty office, Harvey said to Brogue, "If you ask me, that skunk will go live somewhere else as soon as you clear the weeds out. And Miss Walden might sell her house and move out someday. Maybe soon—you never know."

"In the meantime," Brogue predicted, "she'll probably stick her nose into everything the way she did today."

"Gorgeous nose," Harvey countered shrewdly. "She's a real knockout."

"You can say that again," Brogue rejoined. Her hot-pink leotard and the dangerous curves it contained still had Brogue panting for air.

"My grade-school teachers never looked anything like Miss Walden," Harvey reflected. "She could be Marilyn Monroe's twin sister."

Brogue couldn't disagree. She'd turn any man's head with her face and figure. But there was more to her than that, in Brogue's opinion. Even though she had talked a blue streak, he suspected there was a unique, exciting woman hiding behind her excess chatter.

Harvey continued accentuating the obvious. "Not many Victorians come with blond scenery of Miss Walden's, ah, upper-body circumference—or with a backyard big enough for a sports court and a pool. Imagine her wearing a bikini in your pool, or picture her in short shorts playing handball with you on your court."

Brogue closed his eyes and visualized the subject of Harvey's sales pitch. He opened his eyes. "I'd have to wear earplugs half the time, Harv. She never stops talking."

"Earplugs would be worth it, Brogue. So don't cross the whole place off before we get the roof and pipes inspected. Maybe they're not in such bad shape."

"Maybe not," Brogue allowed, thinking about Tomasina.

A sixth sense had tipped him off right away that someone had been spying on Harvey and him. He hadn't imagined it would be the schoolteacher who'd been fueling his sex fantasies for two weeks, ever since the crime prevention talk. He'd daydreamed about her every day, even though he wasn't the daydreaming type.

"As far as the ghost goes, you're not a believer," Harvey persisted, "so that's no reason not to buy."

"No good reason," Brogue agreed.

Harvey waggled his eyebrows. "And as for the never-ending legs next door..."

"You're one hell of a salesman, Harv."

"If you're not thinking with your brain cells, Brogue, I don't blame you one bit."

Brogue gave him a hard-boiled, street-savvy grin. "Bye-bye, brain. Hello, neighbor."

"You still want to buy, then?"

"I still do," Brogue confirmed. "The backyard alone makes that place a good investment. But even so, I'm leery of a house that might need major repairs. So how about an inexpensive option to buy?"

"An option for how long?" Harvey wanted to know.

"Three weeks?" Brogue suggested. "Four? However long it would take to double-check the leaks and pipes, get the whole structure evaluated and rule out any high-cost problems."

"I guess we could write up an option offer based on those terms," Harvey said.

"If the place checks out during the option period, Harvey, I'll exercise the option before it expires. Bottom line, I want that big backyard."

Harvey was all smiles. "I'll get the leaks and pipes looked at ASAP so you'll know what you've got on your hands—besides a knockout next door."

TOMASINA COULDN'T BELIEVE her eyes the next morning when she glanced out the window and saw Harvey

Grant attaching a Sale Pending notice to the realty sign in front of Kat's house.

She rushed out in her chenille bathrobe and her slippers and sped down the front steps. "Yoo-hoo, Mr. Grant!"

He turned from his task and looked supremely pleased to see her. "Good morning, Miss Walden."

"What on earth are you doing?" she said, frowning at his smile and the sign.

"Selling the house to Brogue Donovan," he replied. "Or more accurately, selling him a three-week option to buy."

"B-but what about the leaks and the pipes?"

"Brogue's looking forward to fixing them."

Tomasina could barely speak. "What about Osgood?"

"Well, Brogue isn't a believer in ghosts, and frankly, neither am I."

Tomasina belatedly remembered to talk like an amphetamine addict, though it obviously hadn't blocked an offer yesterday. Maybe it would tip the scales today and cause Grant to think twice, for the good of his client. "Kat wasn't a believer, either, Mr. Grant, before Osgood. And I can assure you she wasn't the least bit senile in her final years. She told me often about Osgood's spirit and how it walked through walls and formed icy cold spots in the house."

She shivered for dramatic effect and clutched the lapels of her robe tight under her chin. "Lieutenant Donovan should think twice about owning a house that might be—well, haunted."

Harvey said, "Brogue wants the house if it checks out to be sound. He's eager to fix it up in his spare time."

Tomasina bit her lip, trying to think fast. Now she'd have to brainstorm a way to stop Brogue from exercising his option.

"Lieutenant Donovan should at least spend a night or two there before he signs on any dotted lines," she suggested to Grant.

"Miss Walden, I'm in the business of encouraging people to buy homes, not discouraging them with ghost stories."

"But as the buyer's representative, shouldn't you at least suggest to him that spending a couple of nights in the house beforehand would be wise and couldn't hurt? What if ghosts *do* exist, against all odds?"

"My client is a levelheaded man," he protested.

"I'll suggest it to him myself, then," she decided.

"Miss Walden, Brogue is a cop who deals in facts, not in fancies like ghosts."

"Whatever his outlook on fact and fancy, I can't help being surprised," Tomasina babbled, "that a policeman would be able to afford a house in this price range. Police don't earn all that much more than teachers do on average, do they?"

She stopped to breathe for a moment, and also entertain the sudden, faint hope that maybe Brogue was a corrupt cop on the take. If he was, and a respectable third-grade teacher questioned the source of his inflated income, he'd find himself living at San Quentin rather than next door.

Harvey seized the moment to say, "He inherited the wherewithal from a distant relative."

"Oh. What luck. Hmm." She scraped her mind for something lengthy to point out about distant relations and inheritance taxes.

"It's a buyer's market right now, anyway," Harvey said. "House prices and mortgage interest rates are lower than they've been in years and the market is flooded with Victorians." He handed her his business card. "If you ever decide to sell yours, keep me in mind to list it for you."

"I will," Tomasina fibbed, handing his card right back to him. "In return, would you please write Lieutenant Donovan's home phone number on this for me? I'd like to get in touch with him."

"Why?"

"Oh, not to discourage him, Mr. Grant. No, nothing like that. Only to personally suggest an overnight stay in the house."

"I guess it couldn't hurt." Harvey wrote down the number reluctantly and returned the card to her. He took out his car keys. "Have a good day, Miss Walden."

"You, too, Mr. Grant."

She left him and the ominous sign and went back to her house, brainstorming all the way.

THAT DAY AT SCHOOL she had trouble keeping her mind on teaching. Her third-graders noticed, but she didn't pick up on that until almost too late.

"Miss Walden," one of her more mischievous pupils asked at one point, "can we all go home early today?"

Distracted, she said, "Certainly. Of course."

The entire class erupted in loud hurrahs and stampeded halfway out the door. Rounding up two dozen eight-year-olds and settling them down again took some doing. The teacher in the neighboring classroom even came in to see what all the ruckus was.

"Don't ask," Tomasina told her. But of course the kids told the story all over school at recess.

It was one of those days that she didn't need on top of everything else. By the time school let out that afternoon, she was mighty glad to go home.

As soon as she got there she made two phone calls. The first one was to a Flying Flowers fund-raiser, from whom she learned that the fund to save Kat's house was growing, but not by leaps and bounds. Tomasina alerted him to the pending sale and told him she was doing her best to avert it. He promised to redouble his efforts to drum up more donations.

Her second call was to Brogue. His answering machine came on, without any polite preamble. "This is a machine," his husky voice advised. "You know what to do."

At the sound of the beep, Tomasina was off and running at the mouth. She didn't stop blathering until after his line cut off.

As she put down the receiver, she tried not to acknowledge that the mere sound of Brogue Donovan's voice had started her pulse racing faster than her galloping tongue.

Damn him! He'd been cruising around the periphery of her mind ever since the crime-prevention assembly, but since yesterday he'd been constantly in her thoughts. Her response to his sex appeal and his dark good looks said more than she liked to admit about the absence of men—and sex—in her life.

Back in her early twenties, she'd spent a good part of her personal time in and out of involvements with some nice guys. Nice, but lacking somehow. She couldn't figure out what was missing, though.

She only knew that now she was content to hold out for a man with a special, indescribable something. It didn't seem to exist in any of the men she met. She hadn't dated anyone for the past few months, though she'd been asked out several times.

The trouble with Brogue Donovan, she reflected, was that he couldn't even be called nice. He'd already shown himself to be a tough-as-nails cynic. Cynics were never romantics, never the type to chase rainbows or be inspired by flying flowers.

Despite those failings, Brogue was seeming more attractive to her than any man she'd met in the past ten years. Dynamically, romantically, sexually attractive.

Maybe her attraction to Brogue was just prespring fever, she conjectured as she wandered into her kitchen to commune with the lives she was hoping to save.

Tomasina had Kat to thank for teaching her to love and cherish butterflies. Kat had also taught her to breed them and help reinstate the local species that had almost disappeared from San Francisco.

Tomasina's kitchen was lined along the north wall with narrow wooden ledges that held a glass forest of jars. Each of the two hundred bottles contained a chrysalis, dangling by a silken thread from a twig. Soon the cocoons would split and reveal breathtaking transformations, iridescent miracles, metamorphoses.

Breeding endangered butterflies wasn't just a hobby for Tomasina; it was also a commitment to nature, as it had been for Kat. Tomasina had another hobby— boating—but that was purely for recreation.

The doorbell chimed, she went to the door and found Brogue Donovan on the front porch. He was in uniform. Tall, blue eyed and broad shouldered, he was giving her the most seductive, most heartthrobbing smile she'd ever seen outside of an erotic dream.

"You rang, Miss Walden?"

Tomasina was so surprised by his presence on her doorstep, she couldn't think of a word to flap at him.

"You rang?" he repeated.

She blinked. "I did?"

"You left a message. I called in and got it."

"Oh. Yes, you must have."

She abruptly became aware that she should be blitzing him with blither, but she couldn't seem to get her verbal ball on a roll.

It was hard even to think straight as his gaze drifted over the blue sweater dress she was wearing, the same dress he'd remembered so well yesterday. He was somehow making a casual look at it seem like an intimate, arousing touch.

He said, "I was in the area, so it was convenient to drop by. Your message said something about ghosts and spending a night next door."

Brogue pictured himself spending a night, but not next door. Upstairs in Tomasina Walden's bed with her and her curves was more like it. Her figure looked ripe and tempting under her clingy knit dress. Her blond hair hung thick and silky, full of light and shine. And her wide-set, dark brown eyes made him fantasize about setting them aglow with desire.

Since it wasn't appropriate for a police officer to get physically aroused on a citizen's front porch, he glanced beyond Tomasina into her house. Wasn't she going to invite him inside?

"I just got home from school," she said.

"I'm on my way back to work," he told her. "I did a school speech again today. That's why I'm in my uniform. The rest of the time I'm a plainclothes detective. Homicide."

He noted that something had apparently tied Tomasina's tongue. Somewhere in the back of his mind the pleasing idea formed that maybe Miss Walden was attracted to him and at a loss for words because of it. If that was the case, he was all for it.

"I'm not here to put you in handcuffs," he assured her teasingly. "I'm just returning your phone call in person."

Tomasina blushed, motioned him in and then proceeded to talk up a storm as she led the way into her bay-windowed living room.

"Please sit down, won't you? I'm sure you're wondering why I called and left that long message about the house and Kat's problem with Osgood.

"But what if it turns out to be a problem for you, too? Kat swore she wasn't imagining Osgood any more than you're imagining me at the moment, so wouldn't you want to know one way or the other before you buy her house?"

Brogue took a seat in one of the comfy vintage armchairs and savored the temporary silence before he replied, "You think I should spend a couple of nights in the house beforehand, in short."

"I more than think you should," she declared, perching on the arm of a chair across from him. "I *know* you should, Lieutenant Donovan, and—"

"'Brogue,' okay?" He grinned, getting the hang of how and when to cut in on her continual patter.

"Brogue," she acceded, frowning a little. "As I was saying—"

"Can I call you 'Tomasina'?"

"Yes, fine. But to continue, I hope there's no law against a prospective homeowner trying out a home first before he buys it, because—"

"No law that I know of," he assured her.

"Well, good, because I know I wouldn't buy a car before test-driving it, and I'm sure you wouldn't, either."

"I see your point, Tomasina."

She stared at him, unnerved and puzzled. "You—you do?"

"Sure. Spending a night makes good sense. Not that I believe in ghosts," he added firmly. "Including Oscar."

"Osgood," she corrected. "Osgood Everett Powell."

He shrugged. "Osmond, Oswald, what's the difference?"

"None at all, I suppose, unless he turns out to be more existent than either you or I expect. His long, lingering death next door was—"

"Are you a believer in ghosts or not, Tomasina?"

She raised an eyebrow. "I happen to be neutral, and extremely reluctant to call Kathryn Powell a fruitcake. She just had a vivid enough imagination to believe that Osgood became a ghost after he died."

"You're sure old age wasn't a factor?" he inquired. "Or maybe Miss Powell just stretched the truth at times."

"Not Kat," Tomasina replied, shaking her head. "She was honest to the core and clear minded right up to the end."

Brogue asked, "How long did you say you knew her?"

"Oh, long before my aunt left this house to me. As a child, I visited Aunt Sam here every summer for two weeks. Kat was alone in the world except for her brother, Derek, who stayed with her between his trips around the world. Derek was quite an adventurer, who scaled peaks in Tibet and the Andes and—"

Brogue held up a hand. "If she had no relation besides Derek, then Osgood wasn't related to her?"

"Uh, no. It was pure coincidence that his last name was the same. Actually, Osgood was homeless when Kat took him in. But back to Derek, who traveled the world over as a soldier of fortune. His biggest adventure was guarding South American diamond mines. The tales he told about his adventures were fascinating—buried treasure, bands of diamond thieves..."

Brogue tuned out Tomasina's relentless sound track and took in her parlor with a detective's eye for detail. The decor was an inviting mix of old-fashioned and contemporary. She apparently couldn't live without books, enough to stock a library. Likewise, she had enough houseplants to start a small nursery business.

He deduced that she had probably read more than a few of the books, so she couldn't have been talking while she was reading. Silence must reign now and then, even though she probably talked to the plants the rest of the time.

Her chairs, tables and stained-glass lamps looked like certified antiques, more than a teacher's salary could afford, which meant she'd probably inherited them from Aunt "Good Neighbor" Sam. In contrast, the beige tweed sofa dated only as far back as a few years ago, and the throw pillows looked home sewn.

The room had warmth, style and personality. Without Tomasina's unceasing chatter, it would have been a really peaceful room to come home and relax in.

Brogue tuned in to her monologue again. "Aunt Sam and Kat were best friends," she was saying. "Kat always saw the bright side of things, whereas Aunt Sam was the world's biggest worrywart. Derek died a year before my aunt, and now Kat is gone, too. I—"

He stood up. "I've got to get back to work."

"Oh, I wouldn't want to delay you with my obvious and God-given gift of gab, which is supposed to be an Irish trait. I'm not, of course—Irish, I mean—but as that old Rolling Stones song goes, start me up and I never stop."

Brogue waved his hand dismissively. "I come from a big, Irish clan and you don't hold a candle to some of the gabbiest Donovans I know."

"I—" she bit her lower lip "—I don't?"

"You don't even come close," he said. "I learned to be a good listener, unlike the guys you mentioned yesterday. The ones who weren't."

He shook his head as if there was no understanding why the average man couldn't listen worth a damn.

For a long, tranquil moment Tomasina was speechless. Brogue enjoyed that interlude to the fullest by gazing at her pink, parted, motionless lips and imagining how it would feel to kiss them.

He had a basic male certainty that Tomasina couldn't talk and kiss at the same time. And since he also had a basic male desire to get her busy kissing him in the near future, he wasn't going to let her gift of gab stop him from getting acquainted with her.

If he could get just one kiss in between two words, she might be quiet. Although he'd pause long enough for her to invite him into her bed, where he'd then do his best to keep her too breathless to utter a single syllable—except for "more."

"Well," she finally said, "have a nice remainder of the day."

"I'll try. You, too." He followed her to the door, letting his eyes track the side-to-side motion of her shapely hips and the play of light in her hair.

She held the door open for him. "Let me know when you plan to stay overnight in the house. Otherwise I might think you're a prowler and call the cops."

"Let's shoot for Friday night," he said. "Keep safe, Tomasina."

She nodded, waved him off and closed the door.

Whistling "Start Me Up," Brogue got into his car and drove away with every hope of making his daydreams about Tomasina come true.

He was only interested in pursuing a physical relationship, of course, as was the case with all his close encounters. Out of emotion's reach. Out of harm's way. One short, disastrous marriage had taught him to steer clear of falling in love. Love and matrimony weren't in his vocabulary anymore, much less on his agenda.

He always made sure not to break any hearts, though, having had his own ripped in two. He always prevented any false illusions by stating his ground rules after the first kiss.

No expectations, ma'am. No hopes whatsoever. Don't even think about parking your heart here.

He'd already had a few second thoughts about taking up with his future next-door neighbor, but her female charms and unexplored possibilities kept overriding reason. And it wasn't as if he didn't know how to stay pals with women after the passion played itself to an end.

He smiled and took up singing that raunchy old Rolling Stones song about what a woman could do to a man. Mmm-hmm. Make a grown one cry, a blind one see and a dead one . . . well, come alive.

So, in the short term, Brogue didn't give a damn that his future neighbor could also make any man wish he were half deaf.

3

BROGUE DIDN'T WASTE any time carving Friday night out of the nerve-numbing overtime schedule he worked. Not that anything could numb his most basic nerve in regard to Tomasina, but now his heavy caseload made him wish he were a cop on a regular street beat instead of the head honcho of a homicide squad.

Like every cop he knew, he had a love-hate relationship with murder—he hated the crime and loved bringing murderers to justice. It was grim, grisly, soul-grinding work. And fascinating, despite the horror of it all.

Brogue never got less than totally involved in the cases he worked on, and now he had three full months of paid vacation time stored up and waiting for him to use.

The public-school gigs he'd been doing in uniform were strictly the chief's idea, as an antidote to a disease that every cop worthy of a badge suffered from: hardening of the heart. Brogue had it bad and the top brass knew it.

He had been opposed to doing the crime-prevention talks for school kids, but Chief Russell had been resolute. "For you, hotshot," Russell had said, "it'll be the

R & R you need but never take. So go talk to kids one day a week for the next month. That's an order."

Tuesday had been Brogue's last school stint. Wednesday morning he was in plainclothes again, meeting with the homicide detectives he supervised. The first thing he said to them related directly to Tomasina.

"Don't beep me for anything less than a mass murder Friday night," he announced. "I'm taking the night off."

They all looked at him, and at each other, as if he'd announced that he were departing for Mars on the next space shuttle.

"Stop staring," he growled, "and update me on your caseloads. Simms, you first. What's your priority today?"

Simms, a gangly type with a military crewcut, shook himself. "I'm still investigating that last drive-by," he replied. "Today I've got five leads to follow up, plus I'm supposed to be present at the morgue to witness an ID on a DOA."

There had been a rash of random drive-by shootings at bus stops in the city within the past month. Each had resulted in someone being wounded or killed.

"You do the leads," Brogue said. "I'll do your morgue duty." He hated the morgue; they all did. This would be a favor to Simms who'd been working his butt off on the drive-bys. "Garza, you next. What's up?"

And so it went, each detective in the squad reporting on status. When the updates were done and everyone dispersed for the day, Brogue holed up in his office, where he phoned Harvey Grant.

"Any problem if I spend Friday night in the house, just to make sure I'll like living in it?"

"Miss Walden's suggestion, I'll bet," Harvey said dryly. "She mentioned that—and made me give her your number—when I went over to change the sign."

Brogue couldn't resist asking, "Was she wearing that pink outfit again?"

"No, a bathrobe. It was eight a.m."

"What kind of a bathrobe?"

"Find out for yourself, Brogue."

"I'm hoping to, Harvey, Friday night."

"You're not spending the night to check out her rumor of a ghost, are you?"

"No way. I want to see more of her and I suspect the feeling is mutual."

Harvey chuckled. "What I wouldn't give to be single and in my prime, like you. By the way, I reviewed the house inspection the state already conducted. Minor leaks in the roof, no dry rot. Any amateur plumber should be able to get the groans out of the pipes. I've ordered a second opinion and a separate structural inspection, too."

"Good. How do I get a house key for Friday?"

"I'll drop it off to you on my way to show a condo at noon," Harvey offered. "Will you be in or out of your office?"

"Out. At the morgue."

"Ugh. I don't envy you that."

"All in a day's work," Brogue told him, making a morgue ID sound like no big deal rather than the short-term hell it was. "Catch you later."

He hung up, closed his eyes and diverted his thoughts to a subject that would be sure to improve his state of mind.

Tomasina.

He started letting his favorite daydream about her run wild. The daydream in which he peeled Tomasina's hot-pink leotard off her body, inch by erotic inch. He took his time drawing the stretchy fabric down slowly, too slowly for her, it seemed, because she always begged him to hurry, please hurry.

For some insane reason he ignored her pleas each time, prolonging the procedure and torturing himself with each exposed inch of her knockout body. Her voluptuous breasts and pert, pink nipples. Her sleek, silky thighs and the wet heat between them.

Finally, he fantasized her wrapping her never-ending legs around his hips and . . .

Brogue ground his teeth in frustration, picked up the phone again and punched in Tomasina's number. He got a busy signal. Tried the number a second time, two minutes later. Still busy. Not a big surprise, given her gift of gab.

He went back to daydreaming about her. . . .

TOMASINA DANGLED her phone off the hook as she looked up the number of Primo Maggio, an old friend of Kat's and Derek's. Known to everyone as Maggio the Magnificent, he was a retired magician who owned

Maggissimo, a magic-supply shop in North Beach. Derek had befriended him in Italy, at a circus performance, and Kat had sponsored his immigration to the U.S.

A charter member of the Flying Flowers Society, Primo knew all about Kat's house being for sale. Tomasina was hoping he could help her figure out how to make the house seem to be haunted.

An unfamiliar, bored-sounding male voice answered the phone. "Yo. What can I do you for?"

"Is this Maggissimo?" she asked, thinking she must have dialed the wrong number.

"Yeah, this is it."

"May I speak to Primo—if he's there?" The only help she remembered him having in the shop was his wife, Stella.

"Who wants to know?" the brash, nasal voice inquired.

Suddenly Primo came on the line. "*Ciao*, Maggissimo. May I help you, please?"

"Hi, Primo. It's Tomasina Walden."

"*Cara!* How are you?"

"Fine, thanks. Who answered the phone?"

Primo's voice lowered. "Rick Solari, Stella's nephew. From Brooklyn. Never mind him."

She briefly explained why she'd called and he replied that he'd be glad to help.

"I have many customers right now, *cara*. Meet me for lunch in one hour, eh? I will think up some tricks to save the poor little butterflies."

Tomasina hopped on a Muni bus to his charming, cluttered, hole-in-the-wall shop. The display window was crammed with magicians' supplies, books about magic, colorful posters of notable illusionists—Houdini, David Copperfield and Primo himself, as round and sturdy as a cask of Chianti. A jovial fellow, he wore his gray, flowing mustache waxed at the ends and curled upward like a second smile.

"*Cara*," he greeted her. "The longer you live, more *bellissima* you get. Hair like the sunshine, eyes like a double *espresso*."

Tomasina laughed. "And you, Primo, are always the master of the charming word and the magic touch."

"So, *cara*, we will go have some pasta—the beauty and the beast together. We never tell Stella, okay?"

"Be sure to tell her I said hello." Tomasina glanced past him at a cocky-looking young man behind the counter.

He was smoking a cigarette and scanning her figure through the smoke. His black T-shirt had a Megadeth logo, his buzz-cut black hair was a quarter-inch long and three tiny gold rings pierced his left nostril. He also had a row of seven small sunburst studs piercing the outer curve of his right ear.

"Rick," Primo said, his smile fading.

Tomasina tried not to look put off by Rick's appearance as Primo muttered a curt introduction. Rick responded with a brash leer.

"You could be a *Penthouse* centerfold easy," he said, blowing a smoke ring at her.

Primo scowled at him. "Mr. Smart Aleck. No respect for a lady."

"Like I should lie about the truth or something?" Rick shrugged off the reproof.

"I'll take it as a compliment, then," Tomasina said to ease the tension a little. Rick was obviously younger than his age, which couldn't be more than seventeen or eighteen.

Grumbling, Primo led Tomasina past his wife's nephew and into the back office. "Come. I find a book for you, *cara*. A book of haunted houses."

The office was cramped and cluttered, utterly disorganized. A desk, a swivel-base chair and an overburdened bookcase took up most of the small room. Muttering in Italian, Primo motioned her to have a seat while he searched the bookshelves.

She sat and regarded the magic paraphernalia and untidy stacks of papers and invoices on the desk. There was a pile of racing forms from the Golden Gate Fields racetrack. Primo had always been a horse-racing fan.

Lying in the jumble was a thick, worn, leather-bound book that had no title on the spine. There were several bookmarks between the pages and as she looked at it, the book seemed vaguely familiar to her. Curious, she picked it up from the pile.

"What's this, Primo?"

"Eh?"

"This." She swiveled around in the chair to show him. "It looks old and interesting."

"Oh, it is only Derek's diary," he said, taking it from her and laying it aside. "Kat gave it to me after he died. He told his adventures there, big whoopers."

Tomasina smiled at his fractured slang. "You mean whoppers, tall tales. I remember the diary now. Kat used to read it occasionally for remembrance."

She noticed that Rick was hanging around the office door, eavesdropping with a smirk on his lips.

"Look, but don't touch, *cara mia*," Rick admonished, mimicking Primo's accent. "Especially not *that* old book." He wagged a finger at her. "Hands off that one."

Primo glared at him, pushed the office door shut and began smiling again as he handed her *America's Haunted Houses*.

"This is the one," he said. "It will put you in the mood."

"I need all the help you can give. Thank you."

"I tell you some special tricks during lunch, *cara*. Let us go."

"Take your time at the track, Unc," Rick drawled as they left.

Out on the sidewalk, Primo stopped to take a small pill. "Nitroglycerin for my angina," he told her. "Rick makes it worse. He steals from me and buys drugs. Each day I count the cash. Each day I lose. For Stella, for her sister, I must close my eyes to a thief in *la famiglia*."

"I'm sorry, Primo. How long has he worked for you?"

"Two weeks. Too long. Like magic, I wish to make him return to Brooklyn." He twirled a finger in the air dramatically. "Poof! Gone!"

"Why did he leave home?"

"Bad friends, vandals, thieves. His mama thinks he needs a nice change. Bah! He needs jail."

Primo led her into a crowded, cozy trattoria, where the waiter and the owner-cook greeted them both with warmth and gusto. Chianti was poured; a rustic Italian loaf was served. After having a sip of wine and a bite of bread dipped in dark green olive oil, Primo brightened.

"Your schoolwork, *cara*. How does it go?"

"Busy," Tomasina replied. "There are the usual ups and downs—good students and not-so-good students."

He offered, "I will visit, make another magic show for your schoolchildren if you wish it."

"They loved the one you did last Halloween, Primo. But something you can do more easily is bring your car this coming Saturday afternoon to the school car wash."

"I might be able," he said, not looking very hopeful.

Tomasina understood. "With Rick to worry about now, you must be reluctant to leave him alone in the shop—even at lunchtime."

He nodded, then winked at her. "For lunch with *cara*, I forget about Rick. Let us speak about ghosts."

"Yes," she agreed. "I need to haunt Kat's house somehow, as I said when I phoned. Otherwise a man named Brogue Donovan will buy it and tear out the garden. Luckily, I mentioned Osgood and convinced Brogue to spend a night in the house as a precaution. You remember Osgood, don't you?"

"*Sì.*" Primo rolled his eyes. "He was Kat's big imagination."

Tomasina nodded. "Fortunately, Brogue Donovan doesn't know Osgood wasn't human. If I can haunt the house in some easy, harmless, believable way, Brogue will back out of his offer."

"This man, Brogue," said Primo. "Good? Bad?"

Tomasina shrugged and felt her cheeks heat. "Good, I suppose, aside from his murderous plans for the garden."

"A married man? Or bachelor?"

"Divorced." She felt her blush deepen. "No children."

"Young? Old?"

"Midthirties," she guessed, her cheeks getting progressively warmer.

Primo winked. "Handsome?"

"Yes," she had to admit. "However, he's a cop—a homicide detective—and I'm definitely not interested. You know why."

"I know." Primo's dark eyes grew somber. "Your papa and sister."

He joined her in respectful silence for a long moment. Then he lightened the mood by teasing her again.

"The rose petals bloom in your cheeks for Brogue, *cara*. I can see them."

She shook her head. "No cops for me."

"You have big eyes for him even so, this Brogue."

"I only want to make him disappear." She imitated Primo by twirling one hand in the air above her head. "Poof! Gone! Tell me how."

"You will need four things," he said conspiratorially. "Perfume oil, dry ice, marbles and Airwick. He still lives, I hope?"

Tomasina affirmed that he did, then listened carefully as Primo explained how she could carry off a haunting with the three items he'd named and a bit of help from Airwick. When Primo had finished, she was ecstatic.

"You're a genius!" she exclaimed. "I'll buy perfume oil on the way home. I've got lots of marbles in my Chinese checkers set. Where can I get dry ice?"

"I will get some wholesale for you when you need it," he offered. "Call me when the time comes."

"Tell me again how to handle the dry ice."

He repeated the procedure, step by step, reminding her to wear oven mitts to protect her hands.

"Thank you, Primo. *Grazie* a million times." She toasted him with her wine.

"I am sorry my magic will scare Brogue away from you," Primo teasingly lamented.

"I'm sure," she said, "he'll find some other house after he revokes his option. It's a buyer's market out there."

"He will never find another you, *cara*. Will you find another him?"

"I hope not," she declared, but she couldn't keep from feeling a little bit sorry, too.

KAT, DEREK AND SAMANTHA conferred about the book in Primo's office. They had trekked along with Tomasina to North Beach for a change of scene.

"When did you give Primo your diary, Derek?" Kat asked.

Derek refreshed her memory. "I didn't. You gave it to him in a big trunkful of my things, after I died. I had wanted my true love, Samantha, to have it. She would have then passed it down to Tomasina."

"I see," Kat said. "I mustn't have been paying close attention when I sorted out your belongings."

"You were distraught, Sis."

Kat nodded, remembering. "Yes, very much so. Like most people, I wasn't sure there was a hereafter. I felt certain I'd never, ever see you again."

"Oh, ye of little faith," he teased. "Hereafter we are. And now that we are," he continued in a more expansive tone, "we need to get my diary into Tomasina's hands. There are several cryptic hints in it about where I hid the diamonds. Whoever figures out where they're stashed . . ."

"Will get rich quick," Samantha said worriedly. "It should be Tomasina, of course, who would invest the fortune in a good cause. Primo would gamble it away at the horse races, and Rick would buy drugs."

Derek nodded. "And that kid is reading my memoirs with a sharp eye right now."

"We'll have to keep track of him as much as we can," Kat said. "He has trouble written all over him."

Samantha sighed. "There aren't enough of us to keep tabs on everyone. We've got more than we can handle with Tomasina and Brogue right now."

"We'll work it all out, my love," Derek heartily reassured her. "Where there's a will, there's a way."

POPPING A COUPLE of antacids into his mouth, Brogue left the morgue and went back to his office and the pile of case files on his desk.

He closed his office door and popped another two Tums. They weren't settling his stomach fast enough, so he kicked back in his chair, closed his eyes and thought about Tomasina again. He got to the middle of his daydream...her creamy skin steaming under his fingertips— A knock on the door jolted him out of his reverie.

"Who?" he growled. "What?"

Kidd Chatham, a vice squad detective, poked his head in. He pointed at the towering stack of case folders on Brogue's desk. "I need the Taylor file."

"Help yourself," Brogue said irritably. "It's in the middle of Mount Everest here."

"Bad day, man?" Kidd inquired.

Brogue shook his head, not wanting to talk about the bullet-riddled body in the morgue drawer. "I've had worse."

"Why am I getting your evil eye, then?"

"Bad timing." Brogue gestured impatiently for him to find the file and leave.

"So, what's the problem?" He gave a sly grin. "Not getting enough?"

"Too much," Brogue replied. He'd sure as hell been daydreaming too much.

Kidd looked impressed. "Whoever she was, she wore you out last night."

"It was mutual," Brogue said, keeping up the macho facade.

"Brunette?" Kidd asked. "Redhead?" He unearthed the file and sauntered to the door, where he paused and raised an eyebrow.

"Blonde," Brogue replied.

Kidd lingered. "Screamer, moaner, gasper or groaner?"

"Wouldn't you like to know. Now, will you get lost?"

"I'm gone, man."

Alone again, Brogue closed his eyes . . . for just a few minutes . . . waiting for the Tums to take hold . . . letting himself fantasize again. . . .

He awoke with a start thirty minutes later, amazed he'd snoozed that long without anything happening to disturb him. Nobody knocking on the door? No phone ringing off the hook? Apparently not. His night off was starting way ahead of time.

He took up the phone and dialed Tomasina, willing to just listen to the recording of her sexy, vibrant voice again.

She answered on the fourth ring, sounding breathless. "H'lo?"

"Hi. It's Brogue."

"Donovan?"

"Right." It rubbed him wrong to find out he wasn't the only Brogue she knew. But then, his last name had sprung first to her mind, so he must have one up on the other Brogue.

"Oh." She still sounded out of breath, much as she had sounded throughout most of his daydream.

"H'lo, Brogue."

"Am I calling at a bad time, Tomasina?"

"Aerobics," she panted. "Workout video."

"Ah. Well, don't slow your pace. I just called to say I'm going to spend Friday night next door."

"Friday?" she gasped.

"Is that all right? I was thinking around seven o'clock. So you'd better not call the cops on me, okay?"

"'Kay," she agreed. "Will you need my key to get into the house?"

Seeing a good reason not to mention the key Harvey had left, Brogue asked, "Will you be home then to give it to me if I need it?"

"Y-yes."

"Good." He smiled to himself. "Bye."

Brogue hung up, stared into space and wondered who the hell the other Brogue was.

TOMASINA COULDN'T completely catch her breath, even after she finished exercising. Brogue's deep, husky voice had sent her heart rate well beyond a safe level.

In the shower after her workout, she couldn't ignore that every nerve in her body was conscious of Brogue's sex appeal. She had to admit that it put her into a spin.

However, he was a cop, a fact she'd keep firmly in mind no matter what her libido had to say about it. He represented an emotional risk that two deaths in her family had taught her to avoid. She kept telling herself that he'd soon be out of her life and completely avoidable.

He wouldn't be living next door, not if she could prevent it. He'd only be spending a night there, and

Primo's magic would make it the weirdest, spookiest, creepiest few hours he'd ever spent in one place.

Tomasina dried off, dressed and phoned Primo about the dry ice.

He said, "I will send Rick to you with it on Friday afternoon. That will take his sticky fingers out of my cash box for a little while."

She said, "Tell him I'll be next door at Kat's if I'm not here at home when he comes. Oh, and don't forget the car wash on Saturday if you can come. Bye."

After Friday night, she vowed, *Brogue Donovan will believe in ghosts.*

LATE ON FRIDAY AFTERNOON, Tomasina was at Kat's house, getting it set up to haunt Brogue. A knock sounded on the front door. Answering it, she found Rick there with the dry ice. His appearance was the same as before—nose rings, ear-stud suns. The only difference was the logo on his T-shirt—Metallica.

"*Ciao, cara,*" he said, mimicking Primo. "I got your stuff here from Unc."

"Thank you, Rick." She had the feeling that he expected a tip.

"Mind if I come in?" he asked point-blank. "I like these old houses. I've read about this one in that book Unc has."

"Book?" Tomasina stepped aside and warily allowed him to enter.

He nodded, looking around with narrowed eyes. "The old leather one that dude Derek wrote by hand."

"Oh, the diary."

"Old Derek had some kind of life rolling around the world, didn't he?"

Tomasina nodded. "He and Kat were unique individuals."

Rick strolled past the living room to the dining room. "Kat was Derek's sister and this house was hers, right?" he asked.

"Right."

"And your aunt Samantha used to live next door where you live now," he stated.

"Yes. How do you know so much?"

"I've added it up from what Aunt Stella and Unc say here and there," he replied. "Plus, like I said, I steal peeks at the diary. Don't tattle on me to Unc, though. He hates me in his office."

Making an effort to be polite, she said, "I see no reason to tattle."

"Did you know," Rick then inquired, lighting a cigarette, "that Derek had a hot thing for years and years with your aunt?"

Tomasina wasn't surprised, for Aunt Sam had confided to her that Derek had been the love of her life. He'd gotten married before Aunt Sam had met him, to a shrewish Nob Hill housekeeper whose religion forbade divorce.

"I think respect is in order for those who have passed away, Rick," she said with cool reproach. "My aunt and Derek were deeply in love, but they lived during a far less tolerant time than we live in now."

He blew a smoke ring toward her. "Hey, relax. I'm not being mean, just honest."

"If you don't mind, Rick, I'm very busy right now. I really don't have time to chat."

He ignored her hint, asking, "What do you need dry ice for?"

"It's for a friend," she replied, motioning him back to the front door. "Thank you for your help."

"Anything for a babe like you," Rick said magnanimously. "*Ciao, buon giorno, arrivederci* and toodle-ooo."

He went out the door, got in Primo's sedan and screeched the tires as he took off down the street.

Glad to see him go, Tomasina closed the door and went back to haunting the house.

KAT, DEREK AND SAMANTHA observed with avid interest as Tomasina finished the preparations. After she returned to her own house, they discussed the situation and decided that Brogue might get scared away for good.

"If he does, romance won't be able to bloom," Samantha said fretfully. "Tomasina won't have a chance to learn her lesson about love."

Kat soothed her. "We may be rank-amateur ghosts, but we should be able to save the garden and promote true love at the same time if we work at it. Derek, think up something dramatic we can do to take the edge off Tomasina's haunting plan."

"If what I'm already thinking works out," he said with an adventurous gleam in his eyes, "Brogue won't be the only one believing in Osgood after tonight."

4

AT SEVEN O'CLOCK on Friday night, Brogue parked his Porsche in the narrow driveway of Kathryn Powell's house.

Soon to be mine, he thought. *Home, sweet home.*

It was windy, not unusual in March, and the forecast called for increasing winds and possible thundershowers through the night. It wasn't raining yet, though, just blowing.

Glancing next door, he saw Tomasina's porch light go on. Then she came out in a belted raincoat and crossed her front yard to his car.

He got out and greeted her. "Hi, neighbor."

"Hello, hello," she responded briskly, her hair blowing around her face. "I have the key for you, and if you happen to need some help getting situated tonight, here I am—your helping hand."

Brogue heard an open invitation. "I need all the help I can get, Tomasina. Yours, too."

"Well, then," she said, "let's hurry in and I'll show you where all the light switches are, to begin with."

"Good idea. I'd hate to bumble around in the dark and trip over Osmond."

"*Osgood*," she corrected.

"Whoever." He took a canvas duffel and a sleeping bag out of the car and followed her toward the house.

"You may change your mind about Osgood after tonight, Lieutenant."

"Brogue," he corrected her in turn. "It's a variation of Brogan, an old family name."

Tomasina was making every effort not to think that Brogue was one of the sexiest, most dangerous names she'd ever heard. *It's just another name,* she kept reminding herself, *and he's just another cop.* If only she could convince herself that every little thing about Lieutenant Donovan was ordinary and innocuous.

Tonight he was dressed in jeans, a checked shirt and his leather bomber jacket. Ordinary enough attire, yet he wore it so well that he made it look extraordinary.

He said, "By the way, who's the other Brogue you know?"

"Other Brogue?" she questioned, uncertain what he meant.

"When I called Wednesday afternoon, you said 'Donovan?' after I identified myself. Remember?"

"Oh, yes, I couldn't quite tell if you were you or Jim Brokaw, who calls himself 'Bro.' You sounded somewhat like him and—"

Brogue cut in, before she could gain any momentum. "That explains that. I suppose it's none of my business to ask if Jim Brokaw is somebody you date."

"You're right that it's none of your business, but I don't mind telling you he's a cousin of mine. Bro is very happy with his wife and four children in Klickitat,

Washington. We keep in touch with each other now and then. He's—"

"Sorry to be so nosy," Brogue interrupted her attempt to overexplain. "But since we're going to spend a little time together, I'd like to know about jealous boyfriends in advance if you've got any. You wouldn't want me getting punched out by one, would you?"

Tomasina saw no wisdom in telling Brogue she had no boyfriends, jealous or otherwise, in her present social circle. The smartest thing to do was keep him guessing, which might keep him from coming on strong.

He struck her as a man who didn't let much get in the way of what he wanted. He was making it clear that he wanted her, motor mouth and all. Talking his ears off hadn't done her any good in that regard, so she decided to stop and give her mouth a much-needed rest.

"I'm sure you'd be able to defend yourself against any jealous boyfriends I might have, Brogue."

He gave a slashing smile and said, "You could save me the trouble by answering the question. Are you private property or not?"

He was blunt, she thought, but he was also showing a gentlemanly consideration for commitments. It made her think well of him in that respect, at least.

"No, I'm not," she answered, against her better judgment. "Are you?"

"Not since my divorce."

She left that subject alone, went up the steps to Kat's front porch and unlocked the front door. "Osgood!"

she called out as she turned on the foyer light. "You've got company!"

She saw Brogue look amused and thought smugly of how much less amused he'd be when he started hearing strange sounds from the attic. He'd never guess that Airwick was up there with food, water, a litter box and the marbles from a Chinese checkers game. As Primo had expected, the playful little skunk just loved rolling them around the attic floor with his nose.

"Let's hope Osborne doesn't mind people dropping in on him like this," Brogue commented dryly as he set his overnight gear at the foot of the stairway.

Tomasina gave up correcting him about the deceased fern's proper name. She led him from the entry hall to the dining room, where she had put patchouli oil on the chandelier bulbs.

"The light switch in here isn't inside the door," she informed him. "It's inconveniently across the room."

He caught the sleeve of her raincoat and held her back. "Do you have plans for dinner tonight?" he asked.

His question took her off guard. "No."

"Good. I don't have any, either, and I'm hungry. How does a pizza for two sound?"

Tomasina hadn't been aware of her own hunger until he'd mentioned food. As if in reply to his question, her stomach gurgled loudly.

After that, she had to admit, "It sounds delicious."

Brogue grinned. "Let's call out and have one delivered. Be my first dinner guest, okay?"

She couldn't very well tell him his idea wasn't part of the night's script, and she couldn't think of an appropriate excuse to say no, either. Why hadn't she thought faster and fibbed about having a dinner date? Too late now.

"All right," she agreed.

He took a folding cellular phone out of his jacket pocket. "What's a good place around here that delivers?"

"Shanahan's is popular."

Brogue punched in the three-digit number for directory assistance. He put the phone to his ear, then frowned.

"Static," he muttered, entering the number a second time. A deeper frown. "More static. Must be storm interference."

Tomasina could hear grumbles of thunder outside, and the low whining howl of wind around the corners of the house.

Brogue gave up after a third unsuccessful try and folded the phone. "Mind if I use yours to call?"

Exasperated, she went out with him in the blustering night to her own house. She hadn't counted on his needing her phone. His dinner invitation wasn't part of her plan. The scheme had been that he'd arrive and she'd immediately invite herself into Kat's house with him. Once inside, she had planned to steer him in the direction of each magic trick she had set up.

Now, however, he was entering her house. And she was belatedly remembering that one of her two telephones was on the kitchen wall, where two hundred butterflies were preparing to hatch. The other phone was upstairs in her bedroom.

Neither phone was portable!

She stopped so abruptly inside her front door that Brogue strode straight into her from behind. He closed his arms around her, caught her balance and his own, then turned her around to face him.

"Sorry," she gasped.

"My fault," he murmured, "for following too close."

Too close also described the way he was holding her. Too good was how it felt to be caught up against his tall, strong, hard body. Too right.

She couldn't help but look up into his silver-blue eyes, couldn't make herself blink to break the bond, couldn't think of how to stop wanting him to kiss her.

She whispered his sexy, compelling, dangerous name. "Brogue . . ."

His mouth slowly lowered to hers and gave her everything she had ever wanted in a kiss. Heat. Passion. Heart-pounding excitement. Erotic, agonizing desire.

Probing and stroking, his tongue coupled with hers, made her thoughtless and breathless until the kiss ended, as slowly and inevitably as it had begun.

Tomasina regained enough willpower to move out of Brogue's hold and open her eyes.

"Well," he said thickly, "it was bound to happen. Sooner or later."

Tomasina stepped back and took a deep, shaky breath. "If you mean there's something going on between us, you're quite wrong."

"There's something," he replied, his eyes narrowing intently on her.

"It was accidental and meant nothing to either of us, as far as I'm concerned." She lifted her chin, strove to look cool and collected.

Brogue folded his arms over his chest. "If you ask me, it was more than you want to admit for some reason."

Tomasina decided there was less use in arguing than in being diplomatic, especially since a debate wouldn't further her plan to guide him through Kat's haunted house. That would only be accomplished by staying on neighborly terms with him for a while longer.

"Lieutenant—I mean, Brogue—I'll give some thought to what you just said. In the meantime, go ahead and make your call." She stood aside and gestured for him to go up the stairway. "Second door on the right. Ask info for the number."

"Well, I'll let you off this time because I'm starving," he said, climbing the stairs two at a time. "Pizza for two, coming right up."

After Brogue disappeared upstairs, Tomasina sat down on the bottom stair and smoothed her windtangled hair. She simultaneously felt relieved, unnerved and mortified.

Relieved that Brogue wasn't in the kitchen, where he would have seen her butterfly hatchery and realized she had a personal stake in Kat's garden. Unnerved because she had responded to his kiss without any restraint whatsoever. And mortified that she'd just sent him up to the boudoir. She had no doubt that he was forming inaccurate conclusions about why she had sent him *there* to make his phone call.

The room was a romantic and sensual retreat, where her four-poster canopy bed was draped all around with sheer silk curtains and covered with a luxurious satin spread.

She could easily imagine what Brogue would make of the seven scarlet throw pillows on the bed. Each heart-shaped, satin pillow had a word embroidered on it and they formed a sentence if they were lined up—A Good Man Is Hard To Find. Of course, they could also be arranged to read A Hard Man Is Good To Find.

Kat had made them and given them to her as a joke gift for her twenty-eighth birthday. Of course they were in the most embarrassing order right now because Tomasina had been thinking about a certain cop when she'd made the bed this morning.

"Tomasina?" Brogue called from her bedroom.

She jumped, as if he'd sneaked up behind her. "What?"

"Shanahan's line is busy. Who else around here delivers?"

"Call Beretta's."

"*B* as in . . . bed?"

"Er, yes." Unfortunately.

The provocative tone in Brogue's voice gave her proof that he could read pillows. No doubt he was stretching himself out on her satin bedspread, expecting her to join him up there for some cheap thrills.

She couldn't fault him for thinking what he thought. How could he help it? Any man in his shoes would have gotten the same message.

"Tomasina?" he called again a few moments later.

She tensed again. "What?"

"I've got Beretta's on the line. Is a combination pizza okay with you?"

"Fine, fine."

"Thick crust or thin?"

"Either one. Flip a coin."

She indistinctly heard him conclude the order and give the street address. Then there was silence. Expectant silence?

"Tomasina?"

She almost held her breath. "What?"

"Is this the only phone in the house?"

His perceptive question took her by surprise. How many men would have asked that, just to make sure there was no misunderstanding? Very few. It said something nice about Brogue Donovan, much nicer than she had ever expected.

She answered, "Yes." A big bald lie, but essential at the moment.

"Oh," he said.

He sounded disappointed, which Tomasina found indecently flattering. It made her feel all the sorrier for accidentally getting his hopes up in the first place. She'd be extracareful not to rouse them again.

As he came down the stairs, she made a determined effort to put the conversation on a neutral topic. "I'm looking forward to that pizza," she told him. "Beretta's crust can't be beat, thick or thin."

"I ordered thick," he said. "Thanks for the use of your phone."

"You're quite welcome." Tomasina hastily showed him out the door and accompanied him back to Kat's house. Before long, if she was lucky, he'd be gone for good. She'd just have to hold him at arm's length until then. If she could.

It wouldn't be easy, for she was as unsettled as the weather. Her heart was still leaping, her knees were unsteady and desire still simmered inside. Something was going on, whether she wanted it to or not.

Taking Brogue back up the steps of Kat's house, she saw that a cellophane-wrapped gift basket had apparently been delivered and left on the porch during his phone call.

"It must be for Kat from someone who doesn't know she's gone," Tomasina surmised, seeing that the basket contained a bottle of Highland Mist and two cut-crystal shot glasses. That particular scotch liqueur had always been Kat's favorite.

Tomasina carried the gift inside and turned on the foyer light again. "Osgood!" she called out. "We're ba-a-ack!"

Brogue made exactly the derisive sound she'd expected. She turned her attention to the gift basket and the message card that came with it. Surprisingly, the envelope wasn't addressed to Kat.

"It's for you." She handed the card to Brogue.

Brogue said, "Probably a joke bottle from my homicide squad." He opened the envelope and read the message aloud. "'Happy housewarming from three friends. Enjoy.'" He gave the card a puzzled look. "It's not signed."

Tomasina asked, "No names?"

"Nothing. I don't *have* friends who send anybody liqueurs and fancy glasses." He ripped open the cellophane and examined the bottle. "It's the real thing, with the seal in place, so it didn't come from my motley crew. Who the hell?"

Tomasina admired the two shot glasses. "These look like real crystal."

"Thanks to three mystery somebodies," Brogue said, "we've got ourselves a cocktail party until the pizza gets here." He opened the bottle, poured into both glasses and handed her one.

Like a good neighbor, she joined him in a toast. She watched him drain his shot glass in one quick, masculine swallow. Nothing halfway about the lieutenant, she observed.

"This is good stuff," he declared.

It was *very* good stuff, and she was amazed to find herself drinking almost as quickly as Brogue. He filled both glasses again and she sipped more sparingly of the second serving. Even so, she could feel the effect of the first shot going straight to her head.

Never had one little ounce of liqueur made her so giddy and light-headed. Mellow, perhaps, but she was suddenly feeling much more than mellow.

It seemed to be having a similar effect on Brogue, because he blinked at the bottle and said, "Wow, a little goes a long way, doesn't it?"

"Let's get back on our tour of the light switches," Tomasina suggested. Maybe moving around would burn off the alcohol.

She returned—a bit tipsily—to showing Brogue the switch in Kat's dining room. The chandelier lit up, and she began giving him a history lesson about the background and composition of the Austrian crystal fixture. Rather a *muddled* history lesson, actually, due to her light-headedness.

She drew him directly under the chandelier and more or less pointed out its salient characteristics. As she had planned, the heat of the bulbs began sending a smell into the air.

Except the smell wasn't pungent patchouli! It was . . . but it couldn't be . . . carnations?

"Mmm," Brogue murmured, stepping closer to her under the light. "That's some kind of perfume you're wearing."

Tomasina turned unfocused eyes up to the dazzling light, knowing that carnation was *not* the scent she had applied to the bulbs. Just to make sure she wasn't smelling wrong, she said to Brogue, "Carnation, isn't it?"

He gave her a goofy grin. "Don't you know what perfume you've got on?"

"No," she blurted. "I mean, it's not—" She broke off, confused and getting more so.

Then she became aware of a sudden rise in the room temperature. It made no more sense than the flowery, romantic scent filling the room. The dry ice she had placed in the airflow registers was supposed to cause icy cold drafts and mysterious mists, not heat.

"Is it warm in here . . ." Now she was even having trouble speaking clearly. "Or is it me?"

"It's us," Brogue replied, aiming a finger carefully under her chin and tipping her face up to his. "Body heat." His eyes glittered with reflected light and sexual interest.

"Brogue, something strange is happening. I can't explain it, but . . ."

"I can," he assured her, swaying on his feet. "It's irresistible attraction."

Her lower lip trembled and he stilled it with his thumb. Then he drew her into his arms and took her mouth with his.

Tomasina had little power to resist him. Anyway, she had already learned that resisting him was no easy thing even when she'd had nothing to drink. His kiss was powerful, seductive, and for long dizzying moments she clung to him, surrendering to the moment.

Brogue let basic instinct dictate his actions. He slid his hands down the graceful, pliant curve of Tomasina's spine and tilted her hips forward against his.

He might be deeper in his cups than he'd ever been after less than two shots of liqueur, but his basics were still in peak form. If certain things weren't making sense, well, when had anything *ever* made sense where sex was concerned?

Somehow, Tomasina found the willpower to part her lips from his and gasp, "Brogue, I'm getting scared."

Brogue drew back, confused. Her fervent physical response had given him the impression that her desire equaled his.

"Scared of what? Me?"

"No, of Osgood, I guess. Don't you feel something wrong in here?"

Brogue tightened his arms around her. "All I feel is you. All I *want* to feel is you."

He sought her lips once more to convince her of his words. Kissing her, he felt her respond to him again for a long moment. Then she struggled in his arms and pulled away.

"I'm not wearing perfume, Brogue."

His brain took its time processing her statement before he absorbed what she'd said. "You're kidding."

"No. I don't *have* carnation perfume."

"It's got to be something," he said, reasoning a little less dimly. "Your bath soap, or shampoo. It's damned well not a ghost."

She shook her head, looking flushed and woozy and aroused by his kisses, yet obviously convinced that he was wrong. "Kat's favorite flowers were carnations. It's scary."

"Listen, Tomasina. I'm a cop, remember? I don't know carnation perfume from daisies, but you're safe with a cop."

He saw that she wasn't buying into his professional assurances. She was still in his arms, but appeared clearly alarmed.

"Let's get out of here, Brogue."

Just then the lights dimmed and flickered. A rumble of thunder gathered into a sharp clap overhead. Then another sound came from above. A rolling sound that traveled around the perimeter of the ceiling with gathering speed.

Tomasina knew it couldn't be Airwick playing marbles, since the attic was two floors above the dining room. She clutched at Brogue and gasped, "Maybe Kat was right about a ghost!"

"It's mice or rats," Brogue surmised warily.

Tomasina heard the sound of doubt in his tone. The lights dimmed, flickered, blazed. Then she heard a rasping, tearing sound behind her. She squeezed her eyes shut, afraid to see what she was hearing.

"What's that, Brogue? Can you see it?"

Brogue's body tensed and steadied. "Yeah. I can see it."

"Is it anything like a ghost?"

"No. It's wallpaper peeling straight off the wall."

His words were punctuated by more of the stripping, tearing sound. She didn't turn to look.

"My God!" she exclaimed. "What's happening here? What's—?"

Brogue gripped Tomasina's shoulders. "Don't panic. Understand?"

"I want out of here, Brogue. Let's go." She swallowed hard against an urge to scream.

"We're leaving." His words and his hands were firm, commanding. "Right now."

To Tomasina's astonishment, he swept her off her feet in one quick motion with his powerful, protective arms. Gripped against his broad chest, she found an instant refuge from danger, a reassuring respite from fear.

A cop, she thought, with amazed relief. *A true blue knight.*

5

BROGUE CARRIED Tomasina out of Kat's house and across the windswept yard to her own porch, where he set her down.

"Go inside. Stay there. I'm going back."

She clutched his arm. "Brogue, no!"

"Just to turn out the lights and lock the door," he said. "Go in. Calm down." He shook off her hand and returned to Kat's house.

Tomasina went inside, but she didn't calm down. Her thoughts were with Brogue. What if he didn't return? What if something awful happened to him over there?

What had possessed him to go back at all? Either he had no fear or he was hell-bent on proving that a ghost was nothing to fear. *He shouldn't be all alone over there*, she decided impulsively. Although stiff with fright, she opened the door to follow after him. She stepped out a few paces, then halted as Brogue came dashing up the steps out of the wind.

"You're back!" she nonsensically exclaimed, reaching out to touch him and make sure he was all there. He was loaded down with his duffel, sleeping bag and the gift basket.

"Where do you think you're going?" he inquired gruffly.

"To help you, of course."

"You were supposed to stay inside for safety."

"Anything could have happened to you, Brogue. For heaven's sake!"

He shook his head and gave her the gift basket to carry in. "Your imagination's running wild, Tomasina."

He dropped his gear inside the door and went into the living room with her, where she set the basket on the coffee table. She took off her coat, threw it over a chair and sat down on the couch to collect herself.

Brogue shrugged out of his jacket and took out his pocket phone. "I'll call and change the address on the pizza delivery. You look too scared to eat next door."

Tomasina had collected herself enough to feel indignant. "You wouldn't eat there yourself after this, would you?"

"Sure I would. There's a rational explanation for everything that's just not obvious on the surface." He put the phone to his ear and grimaced. "Static interference."

"Brogue, my imagination didn't create that carnation smell. Or the weird sound. Or the peeling wallpaper."

"What happened," he retorted, "wasn't Osmond."

"Os*good*."

Brogue gave her a fed-up look and folded the phone. "I need yours again."

"You know where it is." Tomasina glowered at him for his stubborn refusal to believe his own eyes, ears and nose. She snapped, "Rather than changing the address, eat next door and split the pizza with Osgood."

"You're too upset to be reasonable, Tomasina." He left her and went upstairs.

Tomasina wasn't too upset to have a sudden realization. She'd better unplug the phone in her kitchen while Brogue was making his call. What if it rang after he came back downstairs? He'd hear it in the kitchen and know she'd lied to him. Then he'd want an explanation.

She hurried into the kitchen, unplugged the wall phone, and hastened back to the couch. Brogue returned a mere thirty seconds later and sat down beside her.

"Called just in time," he said. "Pizza's on its way, due in five minutes." He studied her face. "Calming down?"

She nodded, even though her hands were still trembling. "More or less."

"You still look terrified."

"Well, I've had a terrifying experience, you know. And maybe too much to drink on an empty stomach, as well."

"I got a little too basted myself," he reflected, glancing at the gift basket. "But we barely touched that stuff, and now I'm not feeling it at all. Who the hell sent it to me, anyway, I wonder."

Tomasina replied, "What I wonder is how you can sit there as if nothing happened at Kat's house."

He took one of her shaking hands and held it. "I had a dicey moment during that rolling sound," he admitted reluctantly. "Then the cop in me kicked in and took over. Besides, that was nothing compared with a murder scene, believe me."

Tomasina watched his fingers mesh with hers in a reassuring handclasp. It helped to be reassured. He had the power, somehow, to make what had happened next door seem a little less frightening.

However, she feared the power he had to seduce her. Her cheeks burned as she recalled the desire his hot, urgent, hungry kisses had made her feel for him. She caught her breath as he lifted her hand to his lips and kissed it.

"Brogue, don't start hustling me again."

"Your hands are ice-cold with fear, beautiful. They need warming up. Besides, this feels good, doesn't it?"

Having already told one big black lie, she was hesitant to tell another. She hedged, "How it feels is beside the point."

"I'll stay here all night if you're afraid to be alone," he offered, turning her palm up and pressing his mouth into the sensitive center.

"No. You can't," she said, even though the very thought of being alone tonight gave her the shivers. His mouth moving against her palm gave her shivers, too, of a deliciously different nature.

He nibbled the tips of her fingers, warming them with his breath. "You're afraid to be alone now, aren't you?"

"Yes, but you can't stay."

"You'd feel safe if I did. Otherwise you'll be all by yourself in the dark if there's a power failure."

He'd no sooner said that than the lights in her house dimmed and flickered. She gasped and clutched his hand, then gave a shaky sigh when the power returned to normal.

"See?" he persisted. "You need someone here with you."

She tried pulling her hand away, and didn't succeed. His thumb began stroking the soft skin of her inner wrist, undermining her effort to resist his touch, and his words, and his compelling presence.

"I wouldn't feel safe if you stayed."

"Come on, I'm a law-enforcement officer. I don't attack people—I protect and serve them."

"You're a cynical, hard-boiled cop who's just trying to get me in bed with you, Brogue Donovan."

He gave her a slow, crafty smile.

The doorbell chimed before he could reply. She watched him leave the room and heard him joke with the delivery driver in the entry hall as he paid for the pizza.

For just a moment, she entertained the idea of Brogue staying all night with her. She'd feel less jumpy then, most likely, but she wouldn't feel safe from Brogue. Her kitchen wouldn't be safe from him, either, if he stayed. One more reason to send him home after dinner.

He came back in with the pizza, asking, "Where do we eat?"

"Here," she said, patting the coffee table. "The dining room is too cold in the winter, and my kitchen is a mess."

Brogue shrugged. "I'm a kitchen slob, too. I don't mind a mess."

"I do," she insisted. "Stay where you are and I'll get plates and napkins."

"Bring a flashlight along, if you've got one handy. We might need it if the power goes out."

"Anything to drink?" she asked, naming what she had available.

Brogue opted for a cola and sat down. He watched Tomasina step, wide eyed and nerved up, out of the room. She had a case of the jitters if he'd ever seen one, and he had seen plenty in his career as a cop. She was going to be freaked out all night if he didn't stick around and keep her feeling safe.

For her own good he'd talk her into it. He might not be able to talk her into a few-nights stand, though. Maybe, for his own good, he'd stop trying. His sixth sense was already hinting that he might get more interested than he wanted to, that Tomasina might get under his tough, thick hide.

There was something different and disturbing about how much he wanted her. He had started out wanting only her sumptuous body, but now he'd begun to appreciate her spirit, her style, the damned gutsy way she had run out to help him.

Hell, if he got any more interested, he'd make trouble for himself down the line. He had to keep a one-track mind about her. If he couldn't, he'd better not stick around tonight.

She returned from the kitchen with colas, plates, napkins, flashlight. He dished out the pizza and sat eating it with her, enjoying himself. All of which made a comedy of the hard-bitten thoughts he'd had in her brief absence.

"I've firmly decided that you aren't staying tonight," she announced after her first bite of pizza, "and I'll tell you why."

He held up a hand. "Let me guess first. You're a nice third-grade teacher and you don't sleep with every Tom, Brogue and Harry. Men just don't get that because you're a bombshell blonde and men all have one-track minds."

"Exactly," she confirmed with a look of surprise. "You couldn't have said it better if you were psychic."

"What if I don't have a one-track mind, Tomasina?" Maybe he was quizzing himself, too, he thought. No, he was just making smooth talk.

She replied, "I'm sure your mind is as one-track as the average man's. Most women are pretty good at reading a man's intentions even before he says a word."

"Sort of like a sixth sense," he surmised. "I've got one of those myself." One he wasn't paying the least attention to, he noted uncomfortably as he bit into a second slice of pizza.

She said, "I know all about cops and their sixth senses."

"All? What cops do you know besides me?"

"I know I never want to get involved with one."

Brogue was aware she was telling him to get lost. Yet he couldn't help wanting to know what she had against cops, even though he really shouldn't care.

"Why not? What's wrong with cops?"

Not meeting his eyes, she explained, "They're risk takers who start out wanting to save the world. They think they'll make a difference, but they end up just being reckless."

"You think I don't make a difference in the world?" He gave her a sardonic smile. "You're right. Nobody saves the world these days, least of all a cop."

"I'm not condemning you, Brogue. I'm just not getting involved with you."

"I'm not getting involved with you, either, Tomasina. I just think we have a mutual attraction to explore a little further. You seemed interested before Osgood upset you."

"You finally got the name right," she noted, without confirming or denying his assessment of her interest in him.

"Yeah, but I don't believe he's a ghost. You do." Brogue observed that her hands hadn't stopped trembling. She had hardly eaten a bite. "You're still terrified."

"You're not helping me calm down," she countered. "Wanting to get me in bed. *Trying* to get me in bed."

"Are you annoyed or flattered?"

She spent a moment deciding, then said with a small smile, "Both, I suppose. I'm also aware that I probably encouraged you a little."

"Probably a lot. It wasn't a one-way street from my point of view."

God, he wanted her. He wanted to stay with her and sleep with her. He wanted her turning to him in the night, whether it was for sex or peace of mind.

"You can stop looking hopeful, Brogue. My mind is completely made up."

He raised his hands, palms out. "Okay. I sleep next door in my sleeping bag tonight, all by my lonesome."

She gave him a stricken look. "You're not going back in there!"

"Like hell I'm not. I'll do some investigating, figure out a logical explanation for what happened."

"That's reckless, Brogue. Risky. Something ghostly—ghoulish—happened."

He shook his head. "Rodents might have made that sound we heard, and the flower smell could be perfume on the chandelier. My ex-wife used to spray lamps with it to make the house smell good."

"What tore the paper off the walls?"

"Time, maybe," he replied. "The wallpaper gets weak—the glue wears out. Sooner or later they part company."

"If it was all as simple as that, why did you carry me out of there?"

He glanced around the room. "There's no place like home when you're scared out of your wits. You were, so I brought you here."

"I wasn't as frightened as you make it sound," she disagreed defensively.

Brogue lost his patience. "Maybe I just wanted to be a romance hero, then." He wiped his mouth with his napkin and stood up. "Good night, Tomasina."

She half rose from the couch. "You're leaving—right now?"

Brogue grabbed his jacket and strode to the door. "I never stick around where I'm not wanted."

He didn't take his time going out. Aided by the wind, he even gave the door a satisfying slam behind him. She could spend a dark, stormy night by herself!

TOMASINA SAT ALONE, in ominous silence, staring at the napkin Brogue had thrown down before he left. He was right about her being frightened without him there, she thought. Now she was far more alone than she wanted to be.

It was like last Halloween when she had come home by herself after watching *The Exorcist* at a friend's house. Every little gurgle in her stomach that night, every little creak in the house, had her jumping out of her skin. By the next day, of course, she had been back to normal.

What had happened tonight hadn't been a movie, however.

I'm not a wacky, alarmist screwball, she insisted to herself.

Yet she was alarmed enough to jump up and hurry through the house, flipping on lights in every room on the ground floor. Then she did the same upstairs in her home office, guest room, two bathrooms and bedroom. She turned on the TV there for company and stared, aghast, at the picture that came onto the screen. *Psycho,* the shower scene!

She switched channels and got Bela Lugosi in a vampire cape. "What's the occasion?" she asked the TV. "Fright night in San Francisco?"

The next channel, thank heaven, had Lucy, Desi, Fred and Ethel clowning around. Much better company.

She glanced around her room nervously, noticing dark shadows where she'd never noticed any before. Then, suddenly, without any dimming or flickering, the electrical power went dead. Lights all out. TV off. Darkness all around. And the flashlight was downstairs.

There were sounds down there, intensified in the dark. The big bay window always rattled in the wind. Was that the jiggling noise she heard? Or was it someone—something—forcing the knob on the back door, trying to break in? Or was it the front door? She hadn't locked it after Brogue had left.

She perched on the foot of her bed and plugged her ears with her fingers, worried about Brogue as well as herself. Brogue over there in Kat's haunted house, pretending he had nothing to fear.

Who, except for Kat, would have thought the spirit of a Boston fern could haunt a house?

Tomasina worked up some courage—faltering courage—to get up and find the flashlight. She felt her way out of her room and then down the stairs, aware of every ominous sound the carpeted wood made beneath her feet. Approaching the front door apprehensively, she put one hand on the knob and the other on the dead-bolt grip to lock it.

At the same instant there was a knock on the door. She screamed and jammed the bolt into place. The knock sounded again. And again.

"Tomasina, open up." Brogue's deep, demanding voice.

Relief flooded to her tense nerve endings and she wilted against the door. "It's you?"

"Let me in, dammit!"

She had never heard a more welcome voice in her life. Flinging the door open, she went straight into Brogue's arms. Not hysterical, not panic-stricken, but needing his strong, human presence.

He kicked the door shut behind him and backed up against it, holding her, cradling her head against his chest with one hand tangled in her hair.

"You turned every damned light in the house on before the power went out," he muttered.

She nodded against the smooth, rain-spattered leather of his jacket. "I had to after you left. Why did you come back?"

"I had to." A soft chuckle rumbled in his chest. "Osgood booted me out."

"He what?" Tomasina pulled away a little and stared at Brogue, although she could barely see him. "What happened?"

"Nothing. Just pulling your leg. It's as calm and quiet as a church over there. Inside, I mean."

"Is the power out there, too?"

"You bet. The whole neighborhood's in the dark." He gathered her into his sheltering embrace again. "Did you rethink anything while I was gone?"

"One thing."

"Thought so."

She admitted, "I can't whistle in the dark all night, Brogue. I'm afraid to be alone."

"You want me to stay, for sure?"

"Yes, but I'm still a nice third-grade teacher and I don't sleep with every Tom, Brogue and Harry. Can you get that through your one-track mind?"

"I get your guest bedroom, in other words."

"Correct. It's very nice, as you may have noticed when you passed it to use the phone."

"I eyeballed it," he confirmed. "But I'm a little disappointed—it doesn't have any ruby red pillows like yours."

Tomasina felt her cheeks flush. She was glad he couldn't see it. "Those were a silly birthday gift, not a personal purchase."

"A gift from . . . ?"

"Kat. She sewed them herself. We were both single, you see, never married. We used to, well, commiserate like girlfriends despite our difference in age."

Brogue knew right then he'd better back himself out the door. It looked as though Tomasina was out to find Mr. Right and Brogue damned sure wasn't the Good Man she seemed to have in mind. She'd made it clear tonight that the Hard part was less essential, but that was all he'd been good at since his divorce.

"Would you stay, Brogue? Just to stay?"

"Might as well," he found himself saying despite his thoughts a moment ago. "Where's the flashlight you had?"

"Where it was earlier. I have another one and a few candles and matches in the dining room."

He let her ease her gorgeous curves and hollows away from his body. Hardest damn thing he'd done in a long time. It wasn't like him to make the agreements he was making; after tonight he'd stop acting like somebody he didn't know.

This was some kind of Friday night off he was having. Or wasting. Not sure which, he took off his jacket and hung it on the front doorknob.

He retrieved the flashlight, helped Tomasina find the other one and the candles. Soon the living room was lit by the soft, warm glow of six dinner tapers.

"Would you like to finish the pizza?" Tomasina nervously asked as he sat down on the couch again.

He replied, "I'd like to see you eat more than the nibble you had."

"Not yet," she declined. "I need to settle down a little more. If I can." She sank into an armchair across from him and sighed. "What a night."

Brogue could see that she didn't quite know what to do with him now. He didn't blame her; he didn't know what to do with himself or with her, either. Looking at her made his gut ache with desire. Her hair kept catching the candlelight and he wanted to touch the gentle fire. Watching her cross one endless leg over the other was almost too much to take. Some kind of rough night he was going to have.

"Do you live alone, Brogue?" she asked.

"Yes and no. I've got some aquarium fish. Neon tetras. It's just me and the neons sharing a basic rental condo."

"Any hobbies?"

He gave her a cynical look. "You wouldn't ask if you knew this was my first night off in over a month."

She nodded as if she had expected as much. "That much overtime must be voluntary, meaning you're married to the job."

"It suits me better than a wife ever did. Don't ask why, either," he warned.

"I wasn't intending to, Brogue."

He changed the subject, fast, to draw the conversation away from himself. "I've got something to ask *you*, by the way. What happened to your gift of gab?"

She shrugged. "Maybe I've been scared speechless."

He said with a smile, "Don't start up again just because I mentioned it."

"I may never talk too much again after tonight," she replied.

Brogue wondered if her noise reduction had anything to do with him. If it did, and it lasted, the world had something to thank him for.

"So," he said, "you teach at Serra Vista, third grade, eight-year-olds. You're not cynical, hard-nosed or married to your job. Any hobbies?"

She nodded. "A couple. I have a yacht that I race, for one thing."

"A yacht," he repeated skeptically. "Your own yacht?"

"All mine, yes. Her name is *Xerxes Blue* and she measures a full sixty."

"Are you pulling my leg?"

"Not in the least. Casey Turner, the custodian at Serra Vista, got me interested in yachts through her own interest in them. What, do you think I'm lying?"

Her tone was challenging, yet a smile played around her lips. Lips that he wanted to kiss again, all night long.

"You seriously own a yacht."

"Very seriously. I'm a past vice-commodore of the yacht club and Casey happens to be the commodore this year." She raised an eyebrow and challenged him again. "Is that too much for a cynical cop to believe?"

"Maybe. How many third-grade teachers and school custodians do *you* know who own sixty-foot racing yachts?"

"None, and I didn't say sixty feet."

"My mistake," he conceded. "You didn't say feet. Sixty what? I'm drawing a blank."

"Inches. I'm a member of the model yacht club in Golden Gate Park. The one on Spreckels Lake."

Brogue had to laugh at himself for not picking up on the clues more quickly. "Oh, *that* yacht club. The one with the toy boats."

"I'll have you know there's nothing toylike about my radio-controlled *Xerxes Blue* or any other boat in the club," Tomasina said half-indignantly. "I built her myself and she's a beauty. The winner, too, of last year's biggest regatta."

"Pardon my ignorance. I've obviously got a lot to learn about model yachts."

"Obviously," she agreed, but she laughed with him.

Brogue pictured her on the shore of Spreckels Lake, radio transmitter in hand, racing a sleek little yacht on a Sunday afternoon. The image charmed him, made him want to spend an afternoon like that. With her.

He wondered what her other hobby was. She had said she had a couple. Would the second one warm his cold heart, as well? Probably would, so he wouldn't ask. He was too warm as it was.

Tomasina turned to see the time on the mantel clock. "I have an early day tomorrow preparing for a school car wash and then supervising it. Could we call it a night?"

"I've got to be an early bird, too," Brogue said, rising from the couch. "Paperwork, a mountain of it."

The moment was awkward and Tomasina wasn't certain how to handle it once she came to her feet. A light, witty comment seemed to be called for, but she couldn't think of one to smooth the transition she and Brogue must make from merely talking together to sleeping under the same roof.

She hadn't changed her mind about wanting company tonight. No. Her nerves were on edge, wary, needy for the presence of another human being. Even if it had to be Lieutenant Donovan.

"Do you want anything from the kitchen, Brogue?"

"Nope. Do you?"

"Nothing." She bit her lip. "Um, because of the mess it's in, consider it off-limits while you're here, all right?"

"Sure, if you're that embarrassed by it. Or is the mess in there something illegal—something I'd arrest you for if I saw it?"

"Of course not!" She handed him one of the flashlights. "Go in and see for yourself if you're that suspicious." She held her breath, afraid he'd call her bluff.

He shrugged. "I'm not on badge time, so I'll pass."

Tomasina breathed again and took up the other flashlight. "Excuse me while I go turn off all the light switches I turned on earlier."

"I'll turn out the ones in here and blow out the candles," Brogue offered as she left.

She went, came back and found him waiting for her at the foot of the stairs. He had his duffel under one arm and his sleeping bag under the other. He was flicking his flashlight on and off like a strobe.

"After you," he said politely.

Halfway up, she remarked, "If the power wasn't out and I didn't have the creeps, this arrangement would seem silly."

"If you didn't have them, I'd be bedding down in my sleeping bag next door. Things could be worse on my end than they are."

"But you could just go home if you wished," she told him reluctantly.

"On a night like tonight? I wouldn't be good company for you if I went home, would I?"

"No." She showed him into the guest room, which had the privacy of its own built-in bath and an alcove sitting area furnished with two oak rocking chairs.

"Everything I need," Brogue observed, shining his light around the room. His eyes swung to her. "Except you."

Tomasina wagged her own light at him like an admonishing finger. "No sleepwalking."

He tossed his gear on the bed. "What about kissing?"

"We already did, Brogue."

"That was hello," he murmured, "this is good-night."

He moved toward her, his silver-blue gaze penetrating her eyes, and she knew she'd better turn around and leave the room. She'd better not stay and kiss him. Not even once.

He was too dangerous and attractive, too much of a hero tonight. She didn't check his forward movement, though, and he took her flashlight out of her hand. He tossed it on the bed with his and then his arms came around her.

"Brogue, you're hustling me again. You promised you'd only stay with me. Not—"

"Tomasina, you're gabbing too much again."

His lips came softly to hers, gently silencing and persuading. She felt his hands begin a massage of small circles on her back from her shoulders to her hips. His kiss was not bold and aggressive, but slow and assertive. Tasteful and tantalizing. Too much to withstand or oppose. Tomasina melted against him and gave in to the pleasure she had already learned he could give her in a kiss. Each time seemed different somehow. More breathtaking, more exciting, more intimate in every way.

"We're good together," he whispered against her lips as he outlined them with his tongue. "We're on the same vibe."

Tomasina couldn't dispute that. Physically, she had never clicked as quickly with a man as with Brogue. It had been easier by far to say no to other men and to hold the line with them. But now, oh, now it would be easier by far to say yes.

So easy...

She touched the tip of her tongue to his, thrilled by the erotic contact, then curled her hands over his shoulders and let him deepen his exploration of her mouth. It was such magic to be kissed thoroughly by this man, and to have him want her as much as his body was saying he did.

He was strong, solid and sexually aroused. Tomasina's senses swirled as he cupped his palms on her hips and pressed his hard heat against her. Male body language, elemental and urgent. Then he slid one hand upward and circled his fingers over her breast.

She gasped, arched her back and accepted his caress for one flesh-burning moment. One more, she thought dizzily, and after that she'd stop him. "Just say yes, Tomasina," he breathed into her ear. "You'll never regret it."

She would have liked to believe him. She knew better than to deceive herself.

"Brogue, I *will* regret it."

"Why?"

"It won't mean anything." She eased away from his caresses and made herself step out of his embrace.

He slid his hands into his jeans pockets. "Does it have to mean something?"

"Yes. For me, it does." She drew in a deep, steadying breath and got her flashlight from the bed. "Also, you're a cop, which I didn't mean to forget."

He reminded her, "Your memory slipped more than once before this."

"I know, and I'm sorry. I've made you think there's more to come, but honestly there isn't. This is as far as I go with you."

"What if I settle for that?"

"We both know you're not the type, Brogue." She went to the door of the guest room. "Good night, for the last time."

He mimicked her earlier warning. "No sleepwalking."

She smiled, feeling somewhat forgiven by his last words, and went to her own room. A few more moments in his arms and she might have been seduced into bed without showing any regard for her own standards of sexual conduct.

He shouldn't really appeal to her, yet he did, more than any man she could remember. Skeptical and suspicious, tough-minded and matter-of-fact, bonded to his grueling work, he wasn't a man she should fall for.

He couldn't be; she wouldn't let him.

Unfortunately, her mind and her body were distinctly at odds with each other about the cop in her guest room. He seemed to know it, too, and also seemed to relish the knowledge.

She undressed, put on pajamas and went to bed. Listening, she could hear Brogue. There was the sound of bedsprings giving way under his weight. There was the tumult of the storm outside, the whisking sound of rain blowing against the windows.

Eventually, after a long while, it put her to sleep.

6

DAWN WAS BREAKING and the storm was spent when Tomasina's windup alarm rang the next morning. She hadn't slept soundly, but it hadn't been a sleepless night, either.

She stretched and peered at the clock radio on her nightstand. The digital display was blinking, so power had been restored. She closed her eyes again and her mind went back to what had happened last night—the ghostly events next door, the steamy situations she had gotten into with Brogue.

It began to seem that he might be right about what had caused the strange occurrences at Kat's house. Something logical, rational, explainable.

She knew she'd have to venture over there as soon as Brogue left, because she had to let Airwick out of the attic. In the light of a new day, it was starting to seem possible that some sense could be made of last night.

Hearing the faint sound of bedsprings in the guest room, she wondered whether Brogue was waking up or just moving in his sleep. That led her to wonder if he slept in a T-shirt and briefs, or just briefs alone, or . . .

She let her mind linger, shamelessly, on the idea that Brogue might very well sleep nude. He seemed like the type. Just the bare facts, ma'am. A sensuous, erotic warmth ribboned through her body as she let her thoughts run wild about him, as she fantasized herself in bed with him.

Her nipples tightened and she circled her fingertips around them just once, very slowly, imagining that the touch she felt was not her own but Brogue's. Just once, and then she stopped, because now was no time to indulge in self-fulfilling fantasies.

Now was the time to clear her mind, get out of bed and set Brogue on his way. Just as she was sliding one foot over the edge of her mattress, she heard the shower go on in the guest bathroom. Brogue's timing was right.

Soon, she thought, he'd be gone. It should have been a welcome, relaxing thought, which unfortunately it wasn't. Overnight, he seemed to have woven his presence into the atmosphere of her house. He'd been occupying her mind for longer than that. Worse, he'd be living next door any day now unless somebody—or something—deterred him from buying Kat's house.

Tomasina washed her face, brushed her teeth and combed her hair. Then she dressed in a shapeless, oversize tunic top that no man could find attractive. She pulled on baggy-kneed leggings and completed the un-fashion statement with mismatched sweat socks and a pair of fluffy pink slipper scuffs.

Dressed to discourage, she left her room and knocked on Brogue's open door. Face lathered with shaving foam, he stuck his head and shoulders out of the bathroom.

"Good morning," she greeted him. "Coffee anyone?"

He looked her up and down for two seconds. "'Morning. Sleep okay?'"

"Not well, but better than if I'd been alone here." Taking great care not to gape at the dark, swirly pattern of hair on his broad chest—or crane her neck to see if he had a towel around his hips—she asked him again, "Coffee?"

"Only if you're making it anyway," he replied. "Otherwise, some orange juice if you've got it."

"I'll bring you both, then. Room service." She didn't want him anywhere near the kitchen. Shutting the guest room door on her view of his immensely interesting upper body, she turned and went downstairs.

Frustrated, Brogue stared at the closed door. He'd left it open all night, in case Tomasina had a change of heart. She hadn't, however, and he hadn't truly expected her to. He had just hoped against hope.

He wasn't fond of the fact that he was still hopeful, but there it was. Even a cold shower hadn't helped as much as it should. Tomasina apparently didn't want him hoping, if the way she'd dressed meant what he thought it did.

So he'd just go climb his mountain of paperwork today and forget about Tomasina. He'd been able to like and leave every other woman he'd known in the eight years since his divorce. She'd be no different.

Well, she would be different, but only because she hadn't let him like her the way he wanted. The others hadn't been looking for a good man; he had always made sure of that before he made his moves.

Yet he hadn't made sure of anything in advance with Tomasina. And look what his moves had gotten him. A stay in her guest room—period. Some night off he'd had!

Hearing her phone ring and knowing she was nowhere near it, he tightened the towel around his hips and went to answer the call.

"I'll get it," he called down the stairs. He stepped right into her bedroom.

"Hello. Walden residence."

The woman on the other end sounded flustered, asking, "*Tomasina* Walden's residence?"

"Right. She'll be up in a minute."

"Who is this?"

"Her next-door neighbor—almost."

Tomasina came rushing in, mouthing, "Who is it?"

Brogue gave a shrug. He told the woman, "Here's Tomasina," then handed the receiver over.

Frowning at him, Tomasina took it. "Hello." She listened, then grimaced. "Mom, hi."

Chuckling under his breath, Brogue ducked into the guest room. He closed his door to give Tomasina her privacy, but he could hear through the wall as he dressed.

"No," she was telling her mother. "No, he's nothing of the sort. B*elieve* me."

Brogue suppressed his laughter.

"It's entirely innocent," Tomasina went on. "I'll explain some other time. Why are you calling so early?"

Brogue was wondering the same thing. He leaned against the wall to learn more as he buttoned his shirt.

"Oh, of course . . . I'd love it if you visited for a few days . . . no, you won't be in the way . . . it's not serious and he's not even a *date*, okay?"

Brogue took mental issue with that statement. He'd been a dinner date, more or less.

"Mom, he just—I can't explain right now . . . never mind how attractive he sounds, I swear he's not my type."

Brogue suspected she'd said the last words more loudly than the rest because she wanted her house guest to get the message if he was eavesdropping. At the same time he was flattered that her mom liked his voice.

Now Tomasina was insisting, "He won't be around for you to meet him when you get here. . . . I'm looking forward to your visit— His name? If you must know, it's Brogue . . ."

Brogue started thinking he'd hire Mom to question homicide suspects for him. She was one persistent interrogator. He heard Tomasina sigh loudly as she surrendered the other half of his name.

"Donovan . . . are you satisfied now? Yes, that's one way to describe his name and him. See you soon. Bye."

Brogue couldn't stifle a grin when she knocked on his door a moment later. He opened it.

"I'm dressed. Come in."

She was clearly not amused. "Why on earth did you answer the phone?"

"I thought it might be for me."

"How could it be for you at my house?"

"It could. When I called Beretta's the last time, I also called work. I left your number for a contact, since my cell phone wasn't working. I can't be out of touch if something big happens."

She didn't look mollified by his honest explanation. "You could have waited for me to run up and answer my own phone."

"Look, I was two steps from it and you were way the hell downstairs in your messy kitchen."

"Can you imagine what Mom thinks now?"

"If she's anything like mine, she figures you're a single grown-up with a normal sex drive."

Tomasina settled her hands on her hips. "Your mom must only have sons, then, because mothers of daughters don't think in terms of sex drives."

"True, I'm the only kid my mother's got."

Her frown deepened. "'Only kid'?" she repeated. "I thought you said you come from a big Irish clan."

"I do, but not the way it sounded, I guess. I've got relatives, relatives and more relatives. At any rate, my mom knows better than to call before noon."

"Whereas mine already has me married to you in her mind," Tomasina groaned, and headed down the stairs. "I'll get the coffee. You keep your hands off the phone."

He called after her, "If you had an extension down there, I wouldn't have bothered in the first place."

She called back, "I *do* have one. It just happens to be out of order."

Nothing like a domestic spat to start the day off wrong, Brogue reflected testily. He was reminded of why he'd stayed single for eight years.

Some thanks he was getting for being so damned noble all night. He buckled his belt and rolled up his shirt cuffs, grumbling to himself about misguided knights and ungrateful damsels in distress.

Tomasina returned with coffee and juice on a tray and set it between the two rocking chairs in the alcove.

"I'm sorry," she said, "for getting my dander up about Mom. She wants to see me settle down with a good man. Your answering the phone inflated her hopes."

Brogue waved a hand. "Don't apologize. I get it."

"Sit down and have your coffee," she invited, seating herself in one of the rockers and taking up one of the cups.

He settled into the other chair and spooned sugar into his cup. "Is your mom local?"

"No, L.A. We visit back and forth. She's...a widow."

"That's tough. Sorry your dad didn't make it."

"It's been several years," she said.

Brogue tasted his coffee—damn good brew—and waited to see if she'd say any more about her family. She didn't, and he found that he was curious enough to pry a little.

"Sisters? Brothers?"

"One older sister. She...didn't make it, either."

"Tough," Brogue repeated. His job dealt directly with death every day, but he still never knew what to say when people lost their loved ones. "Your mom gets lonely, then."

She nodded. "I enjoy her visits, despite her occasional nagging. I'm her only chance to be the mother of the bride."

Tomasina glanced at Brogue over the rim of her cup. She knew she was telling him a bit too much on a personal level. She wasn't sure why she didn't just hurry him through his coffee and prompt him to leave. He'd start to think she was lonely. And maybe she was, a little bit, but not enough to justify keeping a cop in the house any longer than simple politeness required.

"If you haven't found Mr. Right yet," Brogue commented, "maybe you're too choosy for your own good."

Her mother's words exactly. Tomasina didn't need him chiming in on the same old subject, as if he had a right to comment about it.

She pointedly replied, "Maybe people who aren't choosy enough end up divorced as a result."

"Touché, Miss Walden."

"You made it easy, Lieutenant."

He set his cup on the tray and stood up. "Party's over. Thanks for the rocket fuel."

"Thank *you* for being good company," she answered, coming to her feet.

He put on his jacket, then took up his duffel and sleeping bag, saying, "You seem to be back on an even keel."

She nodded. "Much better. You're probably right about there being a rational explanation."

"More than probably," he said, going down the stairs behind her. "If I had time today, I'd prove it to you."

"I'll prove it to myself after the car wash."

"Where is it, by the way?"

"At the school parking lot. Why?"

"Just wondering. If I had time—which I don't—I'd drive by and show some school spirit."

She went out on the front porch with him and glanced next door. "For a man with no time, Brogue, your bid to buy Kat's house isn't sensible. Handyman repairs take time you apparently don't have."

"The whole idea of the house," Brogue replied, "is to make me take time. Otherwise, I'll—" He hesitated at the top of the steps and frowned.

"You'll what?"

"Burn out on homicide. That's what."

"I see," Tomasina murmured.

She understood that he was trying to save his life by having a house that needed him. Fixing it up would give him the outside activity he didn't have. The pool and sports court he wanted would provide exercise and recreation.

Tomasina felt torn between what he needed and her promise to Kat. She almost wished he hadn't confided his reasons. It had been better not to know.

"Funny," he said slowly, "I've never put that in words until now."

She saw a look of surprise and wariness in his eyes. It told her he wasn't accustomed to letting anyone know what he thought about himself. As the first one to hear the words he'd said, she felt privileged.

Privileged and special.

He'd shared a part of himself with her. A small part, to be sure, but still a part. It added to what she knew of him—added maybe a little too much.

"You haven't changed your mind about wanting the house, then," she said, giving herself a mental shake back to the problem she still hadn't solved.

"No. I don't buy into the ghost stories you've heard. The only mystery is how we got so looped on so little Highland Mist."

"Oh! Don't forget your basket," she said, remembering it was still inside.

"Keep it. I owe you, anyway, for getting your mom overexcited." He started down the steps.

She had an urge to keep him there for just a moment longer. "Brogue..."

"Yeah?" He turned halfway down.

"You'd make the kids' day if you stopped by the car wash in a squad car. Wearing your uniform." Ridiculous to be saying that to a man she should be hoping not to see again.

He gave her one of the narrow, assessing looks that made her think he never believed anything anyone told him.

"Would it make your day, too, Tomasina?"

"I'm thinking of the kids, Brogue."

He said, "I'd want something in exchange for my valuable time."

"Such as...?"

"You'll find out if I drop by."

He crossed the yard, got in his Porsche and beeped the horn at her as he drove away.

"WHAT AN UNFORTUNATE day for a school car wash," Samantha commented to Kat and Derek as they all hovered over Kat's porch, watching Brogue leave. "Nobody needs a wash after last night's downpour. The school won't make any money now."

Kat saw the bright side, as usual. "What a convenient storm. All that howling wind and crashing thunder rolled in at just the right time. Even I couldn't have imagined a better background than that for the tricks we played on Tomasina."

"I wish," Samantha said, "that we could have played them without frightening her. But then, Brogue's protective instincts wouldn't have risen as mightily as they did, so I suppose it was necessary."

"Tomasina looks like she's back to normal this morning." Derek glanced over to where she stood on her own porch. "Except for that ratty outfit she's wearing. Where did she dig up those clothes?"

"Brogue saw right through it. I'm quite sure he's hooked no matter what she wears," Kat said.

Samantha nodded. "I agree. He wouldn't believe us for a minute, though, if we told him." She shot a teasing look at Derek. "Men."

Derek gave her a kiss. "Women. You wouldn't do any better telling Tomasina that she's as hooked as Brogue."

"They are both in denial and still have a long way to go," Kat decided. "We have our work cut out for us."

"Do we ever," Samantha agreed. "One dark and stormy night has not taught Tomasina the law of true love. Nor has it saved your butterfly garden or brought Derek's treasure to light."

They all watched Tomasina lean over the rail of the porch to have a last, lingering glimpse at Brogue's car.

Kat beamed. "Look at that hopeful little smile on her lips, Sam."

"Yes. It shows how downhearted she'll be if Brogue doesn't show up at the car wash. How sad it will be if he lets them all down, which he might, I'm afraid."

As they watched her, Tomasina took the key to Kat's house out of her tunic pocket. She glanced over at them—not seeing them, of course—and frowned.

"Here she comes to let Airwick out of the attic." They followed her into Kat's house.

"Poor thing," Samantha said. "She's tiptoeing as if there's something to be afraid of. If only we could have frightened her less last night."

They trailed her into the dining room and watched her stare at the panel of wallpaper they'd peeled halfway down the wall.

"That was the hardest part," Derek remarked, as if she could hear him. "It took the three of us together to pull it off."

Tomasina turned and looked up at the chandelier. She moved tentatively to turn it on.

"Go ahead, dear," Kat prompted, even though she knew she couldn't be heard by mortal ears. Except, that is, when it was absolutely necessary to be heard. Their phone call to the gift basket company had been a necessity. Special permission from the highest authority had allowed the gift to be charged to a multibillionaire's credit card number. The billionaire apparently owed someone up there a very small favor.

Tomasina flipped the light switch and soon the pungent scent of patchouli laced the air. "Not carnations after all," she murmured.

"Not now," Samantha affirmed. She nudged Kat. "The pixie dust you sprinkled in their drinks was just the right touch."

Kat preened. "Bless the pixies for supplying it."

Tomasina moved tentatively to an air register and held her hand outstretched over it.

"The warmth you felt was the three of us breathing as hard as we could," Derek informed her.

They watched Tomasina shake her head in confusion. She shrugged after a few moments, then went up to the attic, where Airwick had spent a dry, comfy, sheltered night.

The three ghosts looked at one another and broke into glowing Cheshire grins. Little by little, things were going their way.

TOMASINA GOT to the school just as the first student car washer arrived on his bicycle. Jason was a rambunctious, hyperactive sixth-grader who was always a holy terror. Naturally, he had signed up for water-hose duty. Squirting teachers would be his first priority.

Casey Turner, the school custodian, was already there. A sturdy, retired Coast Guard officer, she was one of Tomasina's best buddies at school and also at the Model Yacht Club, where Casey was the commodore. She had all the car-washing equipment ready—hoses, buckets, sponges and squeegees.

Tomasina greeted her with a warm smile, and Jason with a look that warned the boy not to even *think* of drenching anybody.

"You dressed right today," Casey said in reference to the yellow slicker and rubber splash boots Tomasina was wearing. Casey looked up at the clear, cloudless sky. "And I don't mean for the weather."

Glancing at Jason, Tomasina joked to Casey, "I brought a straitjacket, too, and I don't mean for myself."

Jason was already reaching for the water hose, but Tomasina stepped on the nozzle. "Hands off until the first car gets here, Jase," she said. "I need you to sort out the trunkful of rags and towels I brought."

"Do I *have* to?"

"No complaints. Come with me." She led him to her car, opened the trunk and put him to work.

He retaliated by going into his Beavis and Butt-head routine. "This sucks. Heh. Heh."

Tomasina was everlastingly grateful that Jason would never be in her third grade again. She was still recovering from that year.

With enormous relief she saw that the two other supervisory teachers were coming into the school lot. The vice-principal came strolling out of the building a few minutes later. Then two parent volunteers and several students arrived.

Before long, everyone was there and the first paying car entered the lot. It caused quite a stir, too, because the motorist was Primo Maggio, whom everyone knew from the magic shows he'd done at the school.

He had his wife, Stella, with him. Thin, birdlike and tentative, Stella was Primo's opposite, and they clearly adored each other.

While his car was being soaped, Primo entertained with a few magic hat tricks, producing bouquets of paper flowers and a real, live pigeon.

He chatted with Tomasina after doing his magic.

"*Cara,*" he said, "how did it go last night?"

She shook her head and told him that nothing had gone as they'd planned. "Even the dry ice failed," she lamented after describing the carnation scent and the rolling sounds.

He looked vastly puzzled. "I do not understand, *cara*. Dry ice vapor is heavier than air, and so the cold must flow down the air vent and make freezing drafts below."

"Yes, I know it's a basic law of nature that cold air sinks and hot air rises," she affirmed. "However, heat filled the room. I felt it myself."

He stared at her, baffled. "Your policeman experienced this, too?"

"He has rational explanations for it—rodents, carnation perfume, effects of the lightning storm. All in all, he wasn't deterred and hasn't dropped his option."

Stella came up right then and interrupted, "Primo, the car is washed. *Finito.*"

"We must go," he said to Tomasina. "Our shop is too much alone with Rick."

Stella commented, "A good boy in his heart, Ricky is. He improves each day."

Primo rolled his eyes and led Stella away to their car. "*Ciao, cara.*"

"*Ciao*, Primo, Stella. Thank you for coming." Tomasina waved goodbye to them and turned a watchful eye again on Jason.

The next vehicle to arrive was a small forklift driven over from a nearby construction site. The kids had a ball with it, and with the jolly driver.

The lift, luckily, absorbed Jason's total interest. Tomasina was sorry when the job was finished. She made sure to stay behind Jason during the washes of the many cars that came in after the lift. Casey joined her, eager to talk model yachts. "I saw that you're signed up for the second regatta next weekend," she said.

"Get ready to defend your all-around trophy this year," Tomasina warned her. She and Casey always jokingly needled each other about the races they entered. "The *Xerxes Blue* has never been in better form."

"Pity she's going to lose to my *Painted Lady* like she did on opening day," Casey jibed amiably. "I've put a new rudder on *Lady* since then."

Tomasina huffed, "*Lady* needs more than a new rudder to win against the improvements I've made to *Blue* since then. In fact—"

"Miss Walden, look out!" Jason shouted. "Car behind you!"

Caught off guard, she turned her head and got the back of it drenched by the wily hose master. She sputtered in shock as water, *cold* water, soaked her hair. Icy liquid ran down her neck inside the slicker and slithered down her spine.

Casey started shaking with suppressed laughter. Giggles and guffaws broke out all around, even from the other two teachers and the vice-principal, who were notoriously lax on discipline.

"You little monster!" Tomasina muttered through gritted teeth.

Jason, true to form, immediately went into an innocent-angel act. "Gee, Miss Walden. The hose slipped."

At the same moment, she heard a siren suddenly start up. She turned toward the sound and saw a police cruiser pull into the lot with lights flashing. It parked behind the last car being washed.

Tomasina's heart skipped several beats as she stood there dripping. Brogue. Then the siren stopped and his voice came over the car's loudspeaker.

"Miss Walden, please bring the boy with the hose over here. Everybody else, stay back. Mind your own business."

Jason gulped and dropped the hose. "Where did *he* come from?"

"Out of the blue," Tomasina told him. "Come with me."

Jason was visibly alarmed. "Is he gonna arrest me?"

"We'll have to see," she replied, stifling a smile as she marched him to Brogue's black-and-white.

Brogue got out, resplendent and imposing in his blue uniform. He leaned back against the side of car, arms and ankles crossed. The quintessential cop.

"Sheez," Jason muttered, dragging his feet. "He saw, didn't he?"

She nodded. "Policemen have excellent vision." It wouldn't hurt for Jason to squirm a little, she thought.

He'd gotten away with too much for too long at Serra Vista. "Policemen know when people lie to them, too," she added for good measure.

"Hello, Miss Walden," Brogue said as they came up to him.

"Hello, Lieutenant Donovan."

Brogue looked at her charge. "Your name, son?"

"Jason Hill." The boy's eyes were round with apprehension.

"Miss Walden appears pretty soaked, Jason."

"Yeah. Sir."

Brogue knelt down to eye level with the boy. "Anything you'd like to tell me about how it happened?"

"I did it," Jason murmured.

Tomasina prompted, "On purpose?"

He nodded and hung his head. "I sort of lied before. I'm sorry."

"You're not going to soak anybody again," Brogue firmly suggested, "are you?"

"No way. Uh-uh."

Brogue took a plastic Kids-Against-Crime badge out of his pocket and fastened it on Jason's sweatshirt. "Be a good guy from now on, or I'll know about it."

Jason grinned, delighted with the badge, then looked imploringly at Tomasina. "I can go?"

"You may. Be extracareful with the hose, too." *But if you happen to turn it on the vice-principal, I'll be the first to laugh,* she thought.

Brogue chuckled, watching Jason run back to reclaim his task. "That ought to keep him honest for at least a day."

"Any longer would be a miracle." Tomasina gave him a wry smile and tried to wring some of the water out of her hair.

"Now who's being cynical?" Brogue taunted.

She met his amused, accusing gaze. "Touché, Lieutenant."

"You made it easy, Miss Walden."

Those were the last words she heard from him for a while, because the kids came crowding around him, wanting badges like Jason's. Brogue had brought plenty of them to distribute.

Tomasina watched him from a distance, feeling inordinately glad that he'd shown up. Her feelings weren't advancing her cause to keep him out of her life, but she couldn't subvert them. Nor could she plug a spurt of displeasure seeing every adult female drawn to where Brogue was. Even the PTA president, a happily married woman, was acting suspiciously like a cop groupie.

He was making everyone's day, Tomasina reflected, her own, as well.

Casey joined her again to help her squeegee the windows of a car the kids had rinsed—and to twit her some more about the *Xerxes Blue*'s loss of the opening-day regatta. Trading good-natured insults, Tomasina kept one eye on Brogue, who seemed to be taking everyone's attention in stride, if not openly enjoying it.

He was hard to read, since he wasn't the type to smile a lot. It made the few smiles and chuckles he parted with seem special. Or so Tomasina was beginning to think.

He caught her eye at one point and broke away from the crowd around him. Her heart tripped on each beat as he started to come toward her.

"How did he know your name, by the way?" Casey asked.

Tomasina tried to sound nonchalant. "Oh, I live next door to a house he might buy. We met across the back fence."

"How come I never get hunks for neighbors?" Casey complained. "He's definitely got eyes for you. Maybe I'll move along so he can make some points with you."

"No, stay here, Casey. Please."

Tomasina was recalling what Brogue had said earlier about wanting something in exchange. With Casey present, Brogue couldn't suggest anything outrageous. If Casey left, Tomasina wasn't sure of her own ability to decline something outrageous.

"Okay, I'm staying," Casey agreed. "But why?"

"Just keep your squeegee going, Case."

Tomasina kept her own going, too, as Brogue approached. He went directly to Casey and introduced himself.

"Brogue Donovan."

Casey reciprocated, giving her own name and shaking Brogue's hand, after which Brogue got straight to the point.

"I'd like a word with Miss Walden, if you don't mind."

Casey glanced at Tomasina and winked, then she said to Brogue, "While I'm gone, don't let her tell you her yacht's better than mine." Casey gave her a little wave and left.

"She must be the custodian commodore you mentioned before," Brogue surmised.

"One and the same," Tomasina confirmed.

"So," Brogue said, "looks like you talked me into more kid stuff, doesn't it?"

"You can't say it isn't a good cause," she replied. She noticed another patrol car coming into the lot, followed by another. "Word seems to have gotten around, too."

"Do I get something in exchange or not?"

She hedged. "First, what do you have in mind?"

"A charity event for you to attend. With me."

"When?"

"Tonight. It's short notice, but I hope that won't stop you."

"What sort of charity event?"

"The Police Association Ball. Black-tie. How about it?"

7

TOMASINA DIDN'T DECEIVE herself about why she accepted Brogue's invitation to the Police Association Ball. One good turn deserved another. But she also had to admit that her persistent attraction to Brogue played at least a minor role in her decision.

So she went right home after the car wash and moved the butterfly jars from the kitchen to the attic—an easy transfer, since her house had an old-fashioned, pulley-style dumbwaiter that served each floor. The new location would keep Brogue from seeing the jars and forming any suspicions about her from them.

She had a firm intention to keep her distance from him, including emotionally. She had handled it physically so far without getting into deep water; she would handle it the same way where her emotions were concerned.

To make certain of that, she did something she hadn't done in a long time. After moving the jars, she curled up with a box of tissues and her family photo album for a painful, heartbreaking hour of remembrance.

There was the police academy portrait of her father, Reece, a square-jawed young man with a set, determined face. Later, a snapshot of him as a rookie, looking tough and invincible. Pictures of her infant self and her toddler sister, Keely, cradled in their daddy's strong arms.

A photo of him, older, an inner-city patrol cop, his face grim and bleak. A snapshot of the family together one Christmas with her mother, Gwen, appearing tense and apprehensive. A family of four.

And then, when Tomasina was fifteen, the newspaper headlines: Fatally Shot In Line Of Duty. Slain Officer Gave His Life. City Grieves. 2,000 Pay Last Respects.

A family of three in mourning.

Five years later, the police academy portrait of spunky, blond Keely, following in Reeve Walden's career path. Barely a year after that, headlines again: Rookie Slain On Routine Call. Tragic Loss. 2,000 Pay Last Respects.

A family of two in mourning.

Tomasina slowly closed the album, knowing she couldn't bear to live through another senseless, personal tragedy. She honored the memory of her father and sister, and loved them with all her heart. Missed them so much. Thought of them every single day.

Nothing would change that, but loving another cop would be too great a personal risk. She would end her relationship with Brogue tonight. She'd make drawing the line her first priority.

In a somber mood, she started getting ready for the ball. Her spirits lifted a little as she curled her long hair into a mass of soft, wavy ringlets and piled them high on her head. She brightened a little more once she was dressed in a sleek, emerald silk sheath that featured a scooped neckline and flowing chiffon sleeves. A stroke of lily perfume here and there had an aromatherapy effect. She was ready for a date and that was all, she told herself.

The doorbell chimed, she let Brogue in, and tried to make light of how stunning he looked wearing a black tux.

She quipped, "James Bond coming to call?"

"Wow" was all he had to say about how she looked.

A low, masculine growl of approval, it made her heart begin to beat double time. She went out with him, into the starry night, to his Porsche.

Once in the car, he glanced sideways at her before starting the engine. He said, "What I really meant was you look out-of-this-world beautiful, Tomasina."

It wasn't the finest compliment she'd ever gotten, or the smoothest, but it flustered her so much that it might as well have been.

"Thank you, Brogue. So do you."

She thought he'd start up the car then, but he didn't. He angled another glance at her, a pensive, questioning look.

"Listen, would it ruin your fun if we passed up the ball and did something else?"

"No," she replied slowly, "depending on what something else is."

"Dinner somewhere really nice, maybe. Just us and no crowd of small talkers."

It sounded wonderful and she couldn't say otherwise. She hadn't really been looking forward to making social conversation in a crowd at the ball, and apparently neither had he. However, being "just us" with him would be risky. The situation would be intimate. She hesitated, knowing what she should say.

His next words were curt, apologetic. "Can it. Bad idea."

"No," she said on impulse. "I'd like that better. Just . . . us."

"You're sure?"

She nodded. "Do you have a place in mind?"

He gave it some thought. "The dining room at the Ritz-Carlton."

"Brogue!" Excitement skittered up her spine. The restaurant was elegant, nonpareil, perfect, if everything she'd heard about it was true.

"What the hey," he said, starting the Porsche. "We're dressed to the nines. Let's make the most of it."

Driving to the Ritz, Brogue was startled at himself for the way he was acting. Until the moment Tomasina opened the door and stopped his heart, he had sincerely intended to take her to the charity event.

Now the thought of his fellow cops going gaga over her was unthinkable. Infuriating. He wanted to be the only guy looking at Tomasina Walden tonight.

He knew he should turn the car around, take Tomasina home, thank her for nothing and stop behaving as though he wanted to have her all to himself forever.

Arguing mentally with himself, he pulled up at the hotel entrance and left the car for the parking valet. Just inside the lobby door, his pocket phone beeped.

"So much for dinner at the Ritz," Brogue muttered as he unfolded the phone.

Tomasina watched his face as he answered the call. His lips tightened to a thin, uncompromising line. His jaw clenched.

"When? Where...? Yeah. Give me ten." Stone faced, he clicked off the phone. "I get a homicide. You get a cab home."

She nodded. "I understand."

"Sorry. I should know two nights off back-to-back is stretching my luck." He escorted her outside and signaled the doorman to summon a cab.

"It's all right," she insisted as the taxi drove up. "Really."

He paid the fare and opened the cab door for her. "Keep safe, Tomasina."

She started to step in, but paused and turned back to him. An emotion she couldn't contain made her frame his grim, tense face in her hands and lift her lips to his. For a fleeting, tender, bittersweet moment she kissed him good-night as she had never quite kissed any man before him.

"You keep safe, too, Brogue," she whispered, drawing away from him into the taxi. It moved on and she knew she had done the right thing. No one should go out and fight crime without something extra to go on.

BROGUE ARRIVED at the homicide scene on Mission Street ten minutes after Tomasina kissed him. It was a typical street scene: seven patrol units with bar lights flashing; fourteen uniforms securing the area with tape.

He recognized Valenzuela, Kantoff, Daniels, Snow, Adams, Culver.

"Oh, my God," Daniels said as Brogue ducked in under the yellow tape. "Who let the penguin out of the zoo?"

The others snickered with him at Brogue's duds, and Brogue let their inappropriate humor pass for what he knew it was—armor against sorrow, horror, death. Some cops were worse than others about it, but none of them survived on the city streets without forming a protective shell around their emotions.

"What's the story?" he asked, eyeing the plastic sheet that covered a body.

Valenzuela replied, "Drive-by shooter. Assault weapon. Two teenage male victims. One done for, one critical en route to E room."

Brogue continued his standard queries. "Witnesses?"

"One, besides the critical," Culver said, pointing to a vacant-eyed derelict. "For what he's worth."

Brogue muttered a lewd curse. "He's *it*? The only one?"

Adams said, "If the survivor pegs out, forget it."

"What are survivor's odds?" Brogue asked.

Kantoff shook her head. "Ask for a miracle and then some."

Brogue slowly bent and lifted a corner of the plastic sheet. The face of a teen, in the prime of adolescence, staring sightless into eternity.

Brogue let the sheet slip out of his fingers. Clearing his throat, he straightened again and rubbed the back of his neck. He asked the silent, useless question, *Why?* and found no answer. Never an answer.

He glared at the officers grouped around him and lashed out. "Goddammit, don't just stand there with your elbows up your noses!"

They looked at each other, fell away and dispersed into smaller groups. Then Valenzuela came back and held out a handkerchief to him.

"What's that for?" Brogue growled.

"The red smackeroo on your mouth, man."

"Oh."

"Yeah."

"Thanks."

"Any time."

"You're all laughing your guts out, aren't you?"

Val grinned. "Every little bit helps."

Valenzuela was right. It was a relief for Brogue to join in and make fun of himself as the other officers were doing. Even at death scenes, there was occasionally a saving grace. This time, Tomasina had unwittingly provided it.

He wiped off her lipstick, but her kiss stayed with him.

TOMASINA'S PHONE RANG the next morning and she knew it was Brogue calling before she answered it. The ring was different somehow. She was becoming instinctive about him, another warning sign not to get further involved.

He started talking right out as if confident that she'd know his voice. "I just ran a background check on a Mr.

Osgood Everett Powell, deceased, and I come up with zip on him. Any idea why that might be?"

"Why did you bother?" Tomasina asked in return, trying to stall for time and decide whether Osgood was worth lying about.

"I bothered," Brogue replied, "because the more I think about it, some of what happened the other night bugs me. My check says nobody died on that property but Kathryn Powell. Her brother, Derek, died at Saint Mary's Hospital. Your aunt Samantha passed away in L.A. at your mother's house. What gives with Osgood?"

Tomasina decided the whole truth might as well come out. She had never felt good about keeping part of it to herself. "For one thing, Brogue, I never said he was a human."

There was silence on the other end for a beat.

"What the hell was he, then?"

"Sort of a . . . fern."

"What?"

"A Boston fern. I told you Kat was eccentric, but I didn't want to make her sound unbalanced, because she wasn't. She was just extraordinarily imaginative and she always named every one of her houseplants. When Osgood—her favorite—died of root rot, well, she enjoyed imagining that his ghost remained in her house."

There was another beat of silence on Brogue's end. "Let me get this straight. You were scared stiff of a houseplant the other night?"

"I was frightened by what *happened*." Tomasina rolled her eyes, glad that he couldn't see the slightly guilty blush on her face. "However, I've been in the house since then and everything seems normal again, except for the wallpaper. I'm going to glue it back up today, since I'm still the caretaker."

Brogue said, "I've decided to sleep there tonight. If something major is wrong with the house, I want to know before my option expires. Don't look for me until around midnight, if you happen to be looking."

She knew she would. "Brogue, I read the write-up in the newspaper about the call you went out on last night."

"What about it?"

"I hope you find who did it."

"No chance of that." He paused again. "By the way, how are you?"

She knew what she shouldn't say, yet she said it anyway. "I'm glad you called."

"Me, too," he replied. "Bye. For now."

She didn't say the rest of what she was thinking—*I'll wait up for you tonight*—because she definitely wasn't going to get any more involved.

"Bye, Brogue."

She hung up the phone and then went over to Kat's house, taking glue for the wallpaper and glass cleaner for the chandelier bulbs. She went first to the garden.

"Airwick," she called, making the little tsk-tsk sound Kat had always used to summon him from his burrow.

He came trotting out, bright eyed and frisky tailed, making his own unique sound of greeting. *Churr-churr.* Tomasina smiled affectionately and petted him, then let him come along into Kat's house with her.

He loved poking around the house and Tomasina enjoyed his company. It helped her feel more comfortable, especially after what had happened. She still had an odd feeling from it. The atmosphere in the house seemed to have changed since then. It wasn't threatening, but it was vaguely unsettling, as if invisible eyes were watching her.

Airwick stayed with her as she cleaned the oil off the chandelier and glued the wallpaper. He trailed along as she removed the dry-ice containers from inside the air vents upstairs.

At a loss to explain the hot drafts she had experienced, Tomasina shook her head. She stacked the ice containers.

"All done. Let's go," she said, looking around for Airwick. He was gone. "Airwick? Tsk-tsk-tsk."

She searched for him throughout the upper floor and attic, then carried the containers downstairs and searched for him there.

"Airwick! C'mon, boy, let's go!"

In the kitchen, she saw that the door to the basement was ajar. "Aha!" Setting the containers aside, she opened it and called him again. Sure enough, he made a churring sound, but he didn't come up.

Sighing impatiently, Tomasina turned on the basement light, went down and found him scratching around in a corner of the storage closet under the stairs. Lined on all sides by built-in shelves, the closet was as empty as the rooms above since the contents of the house had been sold to pay back taxes on the property.

She saw that Airwick had worked one of his front paws into a narrow crack where the walls and floor met in the corner. He'd apparently gotten the paw stuck and seemed unable to pull it out.

"Here, little guy, let me help." Kneeling, she wormed her index finger into the crack alongside his paw. She could feel that he'd gotten it snagged on a piece of metal. To her searching finger, it felt like a small lever of some sort. She wiggled it to loosen his foot and he suddenly came free.

Just as suddenly, one shelf-lined wall of the closet advanced toward her.

Tomasina jumped back, heart in her throat. Astonished, she saw that the wall was moving out from one side, like a door. Without making a sound, it swung open as if she'd said, "Open Sesame."

"What on earth . . . ?" she murmured, too stunned to move.

She was staring into a dark, damp-smelling cavern. Or was it a tunnel? In the dim basement light she couldn't see very far or very clearly.

Airwick made a sharp, excited sound and darted into the opening. Appalled, she saw him dash into the darkness. He glanced back at her, his eyes reflecting the available light.

"Airwick! No! Come back here!"

He ignored orders and ran farther in, out of sight. Tomasina faltered back another step and began to absorb what she had discovered. A cavern—or tunnel— under Kat's house. A secret, for Kat had never said boo about it. From what Tomasina could see, the underground area led in the direction of her own house.

A dark, spooky, earth-and-mildew-smelling place.

Questions and primitive fears filled her mind. What was in there? How far underground did it extend? Why was it there in the first place?

She called to Airwick again and heard the dull, hollow echo of her voice. Again, the skunk replied with his unique little sound, but he didn't return to her. She'd have to get him out somehow.

Calming down from her initial alarm, she decided she'd better investigate—at least by shining a flashlight in there. Maybe Kat had used the space for storage of some sort. Come to think of it, Kat had been eccentric enough that this wasn't quite as surprising as it had seemed at first. It could be that Airwick had been down here with Kat before, since he hadn't hesitated to run right in.

Tomasina tentatively pushed the door to a full open position. She saw that it moved on cleverly concealed hinges that were shiny with oil. Kat must have maintained the door.

Tomasina leaned into the opening and strained to see where it led. As her eyes began to adjust, she made out the outline of wooden supports above and on the sides. It *was* a tunnel, resembling a mine shaft. It looked high enough to walk through upright. But she needed more light to see clearly.

She hurried home to get a flashlight. While she was there, a fascinating question popped into her mind. To find the answer, she ran down to her own basement closet. It was identical to Kat's, since the houses had been built at the same time, according to the same floor plan.

She quickly moved what was stored there, then went down on hands and knees checking the corners for cracks.

Yes! In one corner, a crack.

She slid her finger into it and found a metal lever. Wiggling it, she murmured, "Open Sesame."

A wall of shelves opened out like a door. And there, on the other side, was Airwick.

"Well, blow my mind," she breathed wonderingly. A top-secret passageway connected the two houses. A secret kept by Aunt Sam and Kat. Why did they have a tunnel? Who built it?

Now, rather than being alarmed by her discovery, she was intrigued. Intensely curious, Tomasina shined her flashlight into the passageway.

In the tunnel with Airwick, the three ghosts rejoiced as Tomasina aimed her light through their invisible forms.

"Airwick, you smart little son of a gun," Derek said. "What would we do without you?"

Kat nodded proudly. "I always said he was a wonder of nature, the smartest creature I'd ever known. He continues to prove his genius."

Although pleased and amused by Airwick's success, Samantha was nevertheless discomfited about something else. "I wish we hadn't had to frighten Tomasina again. Poor thing, it's been one strain after another on her nerves."

"Hair-raising experiences build nerve," Derek heartily maintained. "Without the scares I had as a soldier of fortune, I wouldn't be half what I am today."

Kat comforted Sam by saying, "Tomasina doesn't look any the worse for it. In fact, I'd say curiosity is settling in. See how she's getting a broom to sweep away the cobwebs at the door, working up the courage to explore."

They watched her clear the webs and shine her light through them again.

Derek warned, "Move aside, ladies. Here she comes, broom, shaky courage and all."

Holding her breath apprehensively, Tomasina took an experimental step into the tunnel. She found that the earth under her shoe was firm enough to hold her weight. Not squishy or slippery. She took another step and found the same footing.

So far, so good. Her curiosity was overcoming a natural aversion to dark and damp, spiders and webs. In the back of her mind there also lurked Osgood. Ridiculous, but lurking all the same.

Airwick went ahead of her, a reassuring little advance guard. To keep the fingers of irrational fear at bay, she talked to him.

"Have you been down here with Kat before? Bet you have. You seem familiar with this terrain."

She could now see through to the other door. In front of her, Airwick stopped and started digging in the dirt. She shooed him ahead with the broom.

"You know what I'm starting to think?" she mused tentatively. "I think I could sneak through this tunnel tonight and scare Brogue Donovan into never buying Kat's house."

Airwick moved ahead serenely, tail held high, like a tiny dog having a walk.

"What I could do," Tomasina continued, "is howl like a banshee in the basement, then disappear, and he'd never know . . . you know?"

The more she voiced her thoughts to Airwick, the better they sounded as a solution to her problem. Kat's garden might yet have a chance to survive.

"I mean, I've got to do *something*, right? The other tricks didn't work."

Tomasina came out of Kat's closet, leaned on the broom and breathed a sigh of relief. Having passed through once, she knew she could do it again.

Tonight.

8

AFTER HIS MORNING CALL to Tomasina, Brogue worked all day at his office. He had lab reports and evidence files to study and memorize for a case that was going to court within a week. His testimony would count for a lot, and damned if the sleazy legal eagle for the defense was going to trip him up.

By early evening his eyes were strained. His mind was blitzed. His gut was in a knot from too much coffee and a lunch too light to mention.

He wiped his hand over his face and yanked open the desk drawer where he kept antacids and aspirin. Hell of a time to find none of each. Then he remembered he'd finished them off last night. He slammed the drawer closed and raked the fingers of both hands through his hair.

The phone rang and he muttered at it, "I'm not here. Talk to my voice mail this time." Then he thought it might be Tomasina. Suddenly he was sure of it. Sixth sense.

He grabbed up the receiver. "Homicide. Donovan."

"Will you be needing my key to Kat's house tonight?"

He was right. "Thanks for thinking of it, but I got one from Harvey."

"Oh. Okay, that's more or less why I called, then."

"Glad you did. I more or less need a break." He kicked back in his chair, feeling better just from hearing her sexy, upbeat voice. "What are *you* taking a break from?"

"My usual Sunday-night routine of drawing up lesson plans and correcting homework."

"Nothing else going on?"

"Not really." Significant pause. "Why?"

He closed his eyes and mentally crossed his fingers for good luck. "There's a café down the block from here. Not the Ritz, but maybe we could meet for something to eat?"

"I would, but I have a pork roast coming out of the oven in twenty minutes," she said. Then, sounding hesitant and almost reluctant, she proposed, "Maybe you could stop overworking yourself and join me here, instead?"

Brogue glanced at the time on his watch, at the work on his desk, at the crime photos he'd seen enough of for one day.

"It's not anything more than a dinner offer," she added quickly.

"You talked me into it," he said. "I'll be there."

BROGUE DIDN'T EXPECT Tomasina to have company when he arrived twenty minutes after she phoned. He expected to have her all to himself, but she had a man in her living room.

Brogue sized him up in an instant. Six feet, 185 pounds, solid build, gold-brown hair, green eyes.

Dressed like a Ralph Lauren ad. Drink in one hand—
vodka, rocks, no twist, he guessed.

Competition? It looked like it.

Brogue hadn't forgotten Tomasina's saying she
wasn't private property, but that didn't mean she dated
only one man at a time. Nope, it just meant she wasn't
committed, which meant she could socialize with anyone she liked, including the man here tonight.

"Brogue Donovan," she said, introducing him, "this
is Luke Ridgeman."

Brogue shook her guest's hand, while irrationally
hating his guts. Comparing himself with Ridgeman, he
wished he'd had time to change out of the knock-
around corduroys and striped rugby shirt he worked in
on weekends.

"Would you like a cocktail, Brogue?" Tomasina was
asking. She smiled. "A shot of your housewarming gift,
perhaps, or something else?"

"Straight bourbon, if you've got it," he replied, determined to outdo Ridgeman's drink.

She said, "There's some in the kitchen. I'll be back in
a sec. Have a seat and get acquainted." She disappeared to the back of the house.

Brogue remained standing, and so did Luke Ridgeman, who settled an elbow on the mantel while giving
Brogue a polite, but thorough, scrutiny.

"Come here often?" Brogue asked less politely.

Ridgeman nodded. "Often enough. Tomasina didn't
say how she happens to know you."

"We met in my future backyard," Brogue explained. "I've got an option to buy the house next door. How does she happen to know you, by the way?"

"We've been working closely together this year."

Brogue got a perfect picture of Ridgeman "working closely" with Tomasina. Damn him. Brogue didn't want him anywhere near her. He didn't want any other male near her, either, except himself.

He wanted to say, *Listen, Ridgeman, I'm the man in her life. Nobody's going to have her but me. Got it?*

He was feeling dangerously unlike a peace officer at the moment. It was as absurd for him to feel that way, he thought, as it was impossible to feel otherwise. It gave him his first inkling that Tomasina meant more to him than he had wanted to recognize.

"I didn't know this was a dinner party," he said to Ridgeman.

Ridgeman looked surprised by that comment. "Neither did I."

Tomasina came back with an inch of straight bourbon in a short glass. "Sit. Please, everybody."

Brogue braced his legs apart. "No, thanks. I've been sitting all day."

"I'm comfortable where I am, too," Ridgeman said.

Brogue ran his eyes over the velvety black pants and yellow silk blouse Tomasina was wearing. He wondered whom she had dressed for—him or Luke?

"Did Luke tell you we work together?" she asked.

Brogue nodded. "Closely, he says."

"Yes. Job-sharing is a collaborative effort, especially in the elementary grades."

Her words altered his first impression. He looked from her to Ridgeman and tried to recalculate. "You job-share? Third grade?"

Ridgeman nodded. "My wife and I started a family and I wanted more time with our baby son. Tomasina needed time for postgrad studies, so we worked out a half-time arrangement with each other."

Brogue felt almost giddy with relief. *Wife, family, son. Nice guy, now that he wasn't competition.* Brogue recalled then that Tomasina had once said she job-shared. He was starting to get the picture. Most of it.

There was now the question of why the family man was here having cocktails with her, but Brogue wasn't going to ask and make a complete fool of himself.

Ridgeman drained his drink in one long swallow and set the glass on the mantel. "Thanks for the ice water, Tomasina. I'd better get going."

Half the question answered.

Tomasina handed Ridgeman a file folder from the coffee table. "Here's my set of lesson plans for the week. I still need to work up a creative activity for Wednesday afternoon, but I haven't had a creative brainstorm yet."

Other half answered. Brogue took a friendly step forward as Ridgeman held out a hand to him.

"Good to meet you, Brogue."

"Same here, Luke."

Tomasina showed him to the door and came back a moment later. "Brogue, would you mind making a salad while I make gravy?" she asked.

"Mind?" Brogue replied. "I'd crawl on splintered glass for gravy."

Tomasina smiled, leading Brogue through the dining room to the kitchen. To forestall any troublesome questions about why she had rows of narrow, empty shelves on the wall, she had lined them with glassware, cups and spice bottles. It looked somewhat odd and impractical, but not enough to provoke comment.

She put him to work making salad while she tended to her own task. Her kitchen radio was tuned to a jazz station—Charlie Parker playing "Birdland," a lively piece.

"Mind if I ask a rude question?" Brogue said, slicing raw mushrooms into a wooden salad bowl.

"How rude?"

"Financial." He went ahead after she nodded. "How can you afford to job-share?"

She replied, "Aunt Sam left me her savings in addition to this house. With no mortgage debt and a small interest income, I can manage comfortably this year without teaching full-time."

Stirring the pan on the stove, she glanced over her shoulder at Brogue. "Mr. Grant mentioned you inherited from someone, too."

"A modest amount," Brogue said, "but enough for a sizable down payment on a home. City Victorians with big backyards were out of my reach before that."

"You didn't own a home when you were married?"

"I wasn't married long," he said curtly. "I don't talk about it, either."

"I'm sorry I brought it up."

A discomfiting silence settled between them, leavened only by "Birdland" and the sound of the wire whisk stirring in the pan.

"I married a compulsive liar," he said in a low voice, breaking the pause. "Jaclyn could lie better and faster than any criminal I've ever interrogated. She was pathological, no conscience about it. She loved lying—about everything."

He sighed roughly, then went on, "When I say everything, I mean it literally. One of her worst lies was that she had cancer. I guess she did it for attention. When I finally woke up to what her real problem was, she refused to get psychiatric treatment. I was willing to work it out with her, but she had her own agenda and wanted a divorce."

"It would be difficult to trust after that," Tomasina responded sympathetically, and also a little guiltily, since total honesty hadn't been her own policy with Brogue.

He acknowledged, "It's still difficult from my side of it. I already had a load of distrust before I met Jaclyn. Cops get lied to by criminals, witnesses, lawyers. Hell, we've got enough falsehood to deal with, without getting snowed at home."

"Is your distrust why you've been single ever since?" she asked.

"It's a big factor. Besides that, the infidelity and divorce rates for cops are off the charts. Why tempt fate again?"

Tomasina was touched by what Brogue was revealing about himself. She understood him and cared about how he felt. It was a nice feeling, but at the same time, she was afraid. Afraid that this feeling was starting to seem a lot like love.

He made a self-deprecating sound. "Funny that you're supposedly the nonstop talker, yet I'm the one telling my life story."

"I'm not usually a motor mouth," she confessed, seeing a chance to straighten out one of her deceptions a little. "It was a nervous reaction at the time."

After all, the idea of him destroying Kat's garden had been nerve-racking. She certainly would never have talked a blue streak to him if he hadn't mentioned his aversion to noisy neighbors.

"A nervous reaction to *me?*" Brogue inquired.

"Yes, to be honest. You're a cop and I've told you my problem with that."

"I have a feeling you didn't tell me all of your problem with it, Tomasina."

She took a deep breath. "You're right, but I don't want to go into my reasons any more than I have already. It's deeply personal and—"

"Like my marriage disaster," he cut in.

She switched the subject to food. "The gravy's done. Salad finished?"

He tipped the bowl, showing her that he was through.

"Beautiful," she said, complimenting his work. "Please take it to the table and sit down."

She motioned him to an antique pinewood dining set, where she had laid two places across from each other. A pottery vase of red primroses, two lit beeswax candles and an open bottle of Beaujolais formed a cozy centerpiece.

Brogue recalled that he hadn't eaten a home-cooked meal since Christmas with his family. He told himself he wouldn't want to get used to this sort of thing. Domestic pleasures...personal conversations...true confessions. He wouldn't want to start thinking of Tomasina in those terms. Not as a constant companion or a soul mate. He'd be best off thinking of her only as a possible bedmate.

In that last regard, none of his desire for her had diminished. If anything, it was more urgent and intense than ever. He wasn't positive he could last through dinner without throwing the table over to get his hands on her...all over her...full of her.

He was getting excited just sitting there, watching her put a plate of succulent roast, gravy and wild-rice pilaf in front of him. Her breasts were round and full under her silk blouse. Her legs were long and slim in the velvety black pants. Her perfume was the same as she had worn in every erotic daydream he'd had about her.

He filled the wineglasses and she filled the salad plates. They touched glasses in a casual toast, then started eating.

After his first few bites, Brogue said, "Out of this world."

She blushed, gave a thank-you smile and started making some small talk about city schools in general and Serra Vista in particular.

The conversation segued into the crime-prevention talks he had done. She asked leading questions, and he slowly began telling her about how crime work had hardened his heart, the reason why he'd been assigned to the talks. He went on to tell her a few things he'd only discussed before with other cops.

"People die for nothing," he heard himself confide over coffee after dinner. "Cops find that out right away. Senseless violence feeds our pessimism, makes us put up a protective shell. Crime after crime, the shell thickens and hardens."

Tomasina commented, "The world and life aren't all dark. There are more good people than bad people."

He shook his head. "If every crime got reported and every criminal got caught, you wouldn't have room to say what you just said."

"Brogue, your job shows you the worst in human nature."

"It shows me the reality of human nature, Tomasina."

He helped her clear the table and put the food away.

"We're obviously opposites in our outlook on life," she said, scraping plates and rinsing glasses.

He said, "Whatever the case, we're opposites who attract. You look beautiful tonight, Tomasina."

She shook water off her hands. "Stop handing me a line and hand me that towel instead, please."

He held it out to her. She took hold and he slowly pulled his end—and her—toward him.

In the background the radio had Bonnie Raitt crooning "True Blue Lovin'."

"Brogue..." She didn't let go of the towel and he kept pulling.

"'Brogue' what?" he inquired.

"You're forgetting I said 'just dinner.'"

He dropped the towel and slid one hand to the back of her waist. With the other, he tipped up her chin. "Did you really mean it?"

"Not entirely." She took a shallow, unsteadying breath. "I was hoping you'd think I meant it, though."

"Why?"

"Things couldn't work out between us."

Nevertheless, he was bringing her closer and she allowed it. The towel fell from her fingers and she came to him, to the coiled strength of his body, to the blue-silver light gleaming in his eyes.

"One thing is working out between us," he murmured against her lips. "We're on a vibe that won't stop."

She surrendered to his kiss, then to his tongue sliding past her teeth. Her thoughts whirled and spun, filled with him, thrilled with him, enthralled by the captivating effect he had on her.

Lifting her arms, looping her hands behind his neck, she gave in to him, encouraged him to deepen his probe of her mouth and devour her. She knew if it went much further there would be no turning back, no stopping him from having her—or herself from having him.

Trembling, arching into his warmth and against the hard length of his body, she met him kiss for kiss and breath for breath. His desire and hers moved from daring to desperate in the space of a heartbeat as his hands slipped to the buttons of her blouse and opened them.

"God, Tomasina. I need to touch you."

He parted the front clasp of her bra and freed her to be touched.

"I need it, too, Brogue . . . oh, yes."

His breath was husky and hot against the skin of her throat. He gave a ragged sigh, framed her breasts fully in his palms and brushed his thumbs over the centers.

She gasped from the pleasure, then caught her breath again as Brogue pulled away and lifted her effortlessly in his arms. He strode out of the kitchen and straight to the stairs.

At the bottom he paused and whispered softly in her ear, "Yes? Without a doubt?"

"Yes."

It was a first for her to be carried up the flight of stairs into her bedroom, where he set her on her feet and captured her mouth again with his. Kissing him deeply with mounting pressure and passion, Tomasina felt his hips angle forward, felt the long ridge of his erection against her.

He pushed her blouse off, then her bra. They slipped down her arms and fell away as he filled his hands with her breasts and circled the taut tips with his thumbs. She closed her eyes.

This was what she had imagined the morning after the storm. This was more than she had imagined, for his caress was firing her readiness to be his, making her want him more than she had ever wanted a man.

"You're too beautiful to believe, Tomasina." He gazed upon her in the light that came into the room from the hall.

Aching to touch and see him, too, she slipped her hands under his heavy rugby shirt and explored the shape and texture of his chest. He whipped the shirt off over his head and took her in his arms, crushing her breasts against him, rubbing her nipples with his own.

"So good," he groaned, "so good."

Now that the moment had been seized, there was nothing awkward or shy about their volatile reaction to each other. She was a mature, experienced female and Brogue was her male equal. When he lowered her back zipper, she welcomed his palms skimming her bottom, pushing the slacks down.

She shimmied them off and kicked them away, eager to bare more of her skin to him. His body intrigued her . . . the dark pattern of thick hair on his muscled chest, the ripple of his ribs under his skin, the shallow dip of his navel.

Grazing her fingers lower to the bulge in his corduroys brought a hoarse gasp from him. He covered her hand with his and led it up and down there, acquainting her with the full extent of his need. Then he led her hand to one of his front pockets. There she felt the shape of two necessities. Condoms.

"Take them out for me, Tomasina."

She removed both packets and tossed them on the bed.

"I've wanted you since the first day," he said as she unzipped him. "It's been torture, pure hell."

"Soon," she whispered, lowering his trousers to his feet, "it will be heaven."

She in her panties and he in his briefs, they fell onto the bed with each other. The satin comforter was slippery smooth against her skin; the seven scarlet pillows were soft against her back; Brogue's mouth was hot and ravenous on her breasts.

He whirled his tongue over her nipples and blew on them, heightening the sensation. Then he sucked, and she played her fingers in his dark hair as he made a feast of her. She caressed his ears with her thumbs, skimmed her palms to the bunched muscles in his shoulders, moved her hands beyond to the broad width of his upper back.

It was then, palms smoothing down to the elastic band of his briefs, that she felt an unusual texture of skin low on his back in two places close together. Two knotted, puckered craters, they felt like . . .

"What's this?" she asked him, fingertips tracing the jagged, irregular hollows.

He lifted his head from her breasts, breathing hard. "Scars. Nothing to it."

Her breath slowed, became apprehensive. "How did you get scars?"

"Bullets." He lowered his mouth to her breasts again, but she pushed herself back against the pillows.

"A shooting?" she inquired, her voice and body tightening, tensing with greater apprehension.

"I got shot," he confirmed, drawing back to give her a puzzled frown. "Seven years ago, during a crack bust when I worked a narc detail."

"Oh, Brogue." She shook her head at him. "No."

His face fell. "You're turned off. I never thought you'd have a big problem with two little scars."

"It's not the scars themselves, Brogue. It's something else." Tomasina edged away from him and swung her legs over the edge of the mattress, avoiding his eyes.

"Tomasina." He clasped her wrist. "Look at me. We were coming on like there was no tomorrow. What's the problem?"

"I've had it for years." She searched for words. "Ten minutes ago I let my attraction to you push doubt aside. I wasn't thinking. I wasn't . . . I don't know."

"Tell me."

"I'll explain. Give me a moment." She stood and shook off his hold. Taking her chenille bathrobe from the chair it lay on, she slipped into it and belted the tie, then sat in the chair.

"Party must be over," he muttered, getting up and putting on his cords. Bare chested, he sat on the edge of the bed facing her and inquired, "Why?"

She took a deep breath. "My father was a police officer, an LAPD patrol sergeant. My sister went into the same line of work. They both got into shoot-outs in the line of duty and . . ."

"Didn't make it," Brogue supplied, suddenly subdued.

She nodded. "You see why I don't get involved."

"Hey, Tomasina," he said gently, beckoning her. "Come over here."

"No, I'm sorry, but you and I aren't going to tempt fate. I'm not going to mourn family or friend at another police funeral."

His face took on a determined look. "Listen, I used to be in the danger zone, but those days are over for me. Homicide honchos don't get blown away. The odds are against it."

"They were even higher against two officers in one family meeting the same end," she retorted. "I don't want more death in my life."

"Your neighbor died," Brogue said. "Your aunt, too. They both—"

She interrupted, "They passed away naturally. Death by natural causes is understandable."

"Look, I have to do what I have to do, Tomasina. I love and hate my job, but I love it more than I hate it. I'll bet your dad and sister did, too."

"You make me sound as if I'm telling you to quit being a cop, Brogue, which I'm not. I'm telling you to go next door and spend tonight where you planned to spend it in the first place."

"Just like that," he said, his voice turning stony. "Just like nothing happened."

"Yes. Please. Forget that we almost made love."

He came to his feet, grabbed up the rest of his clothes and headed for the bedroom door. "Don't kid yourself that love had anything to do with it."

9

AFTER BROGUE LEFT, Tomasina leveled herself out by having a cup of herbal tea. Sipping it, she peeked through her bedroom curtains and watched Kat's house.

Brogue's car was in the driveway, so she assumed he was indeed spending the night as he had said he would.

She could see lights go on and off as he moved throughout the house. He had them on in the dining room for several minutes, probably while he inspected the chandelier and the wallpaper repair.

Watching, she was able to trace his movements from downstairs to upstairs. Bathroom light on, then off. Last, the light went on in the biggest second-floor bedroom.

Tomasina pictured him unrolling his sleeping bag, getting into it—maybe nude, maybe still magnificently aroused. It didn't seem doubtful, since her own body remained tumid and melting with sexual need. The tea wasn't leveling everything out, especially not her feeling that she should never have lost her head with him. So she peered through the curtains until the lights were out and she was sure Brogue was settled and asleep. She would sneak through the tunnel later tonight and scare him off for good.

IT'S A DAMN GOOD THING you're cynical and thick-skinned, Brogue reflected as he bedded down in his sleeping bag. *Good that you didn't care about having anything but sex with Tomasina tonight.*

That way, he only had to deal with sexual frustration. That way, his emotional frustration stayed out of it. Feeling sympathy for her wouldn't do him a damn bit of good, either, even though he now had an understanding of her problem with him.

She'd lost her father, lost her sister—both cops. He could feel her loss, without any emotional distance from it, since he'd almost suffered their fate himself.

Hell, he should have known better than to get mixed up with a next-door neighbor. He should have stayed at work tonight and kept his nose in the caseload instead of sniffing around Tomasina.

He could still smell her exotic, erotic perfume on his skin, still taste her succulent mouth. There'd be no forgetting the abundant weight of her breasts in his hands, or the berry shape of her nipples against his tongue.

Damn! Powerless to find a comfortable spot on his air mattress, he recalled Tomasina promising him heaven.

He'd need a miracle to get there now. And, heaven help him, he was hoping for one.

IT WAS half past midnight.

Dressed in jeans and a sweatshirt, Tomasina went down to her basement and released the hidden latch in the storage closet. The secret door swung open as before, without a sound. She shined her light into the tunnel and nervously passed to the other end.

Cold. Damp. Creepy. Silent as a grave.

It wasn't easy to put every ghost story she knew out of her mind. From Edgar Allan Poe to Stephen King, she was familiar with so many tales from the dark side. And she had just recently read the book Primo had loaned her about haunted houses.

The chapter titles alone were enough to give anyone goose bumps: "The San Francisco Ghost Bride," "The Dying Gasp," "The Ghosts in the Basement."

Again she felt Osgood lurking in the dark shadows of her mind. Earlier, when Airwick had been with her, the tunnel hadn't seemed as gravelike and claustrophobic as it did now. However, she hadn't been traveling through on a mission to scare the wits out of Brogue Donovan at the time, either.

Poor Brogue. She really regretted having to do this to him. Terrorism was entirely unnatural behavior for her, but what else was left for her to do? Opportunity was at hand, the time was right and necessity was calling at the top of its lungs.

Tomasina came to the end of the tunnel, slowly released the trip latch on the tunnel side of the door and whispered, "Open Sesame."

BROGUE WAS DEEP in a dream, one not unlike his favorite daydream about Tomasina, except tonight she was wearing a see-through, skintight, yellow, silk minidress.

She was unzipping his sleeping bag and whispering, "My wild Irish Brogue . . . let's make some heaven on Earth."

Oh, man, she had nothing on under the dress. He could see everything through the sheer silk. The dark pink tips of her bountiful breasts, the triangle of lacy curls between her thighs. Her hair was a cascade of blond, ruffled at the ends by a slight, fragrant breeze.

She was uncovering him, laying him bare, finding what she sought. Her fingers played provocatively over his chest and then played the same way upon her own breasts. The tip of her tongue peeked out between her full, pouty lips and her pearly white teeth.

She was so good—she was so bad.

Her touch returned to him, drifting down from his nipples to his navel to his avid interest in her. Kneeling between his outspread thighs, fascinated by his strength and size, she bent low and encircled him with her lips, stroked him with her tongue.

He was clenching his fingers in her hair, drawing her up over him, turning her onto her back, spreading her legs. She was wet and hot and whispering his name.

Heaven and Earth. He was loving it, loving her, he was . . .

Awake to a bone-chilling howl in the night!

AaaaaOOOoooOOOooo!

His blood ran cold.

OwwwweeeeeeeEEEE!

His eyes sprang open. The sound came from down below, inside the house.

His adrenaline surged. He kicked reflexively into action. Out of the sleeping bag, gun in right hand. Cell phone in left hand. Move to the sound, ready for anything. Halt and listen. Silence below. Step down the stairs. Ease into the kitchen. Speak into silence.

"Police! Who's there?"

Halt and listen. Silence.

Ease down to the basement. Locate the light switch. "Police!"

Lights on. Nothing. Nobody. Storage closet? *Nada.* Basement windows? Locked inside.

Total silence.

What the hell?

He double-checked the whole basement again. Zero. Same story in the kitchen. Same story, room by room, all through the house.

God, had he somehow dreamed the screaming howls rather than heard them? Had they sounded outside the house instead of inside? Had that fantastic dream simply tricked all of his senses? Had anyone else heard anything? Tomasina?

He unfolded his phone and punched in her number. It rang four times, then switched to her answering machine. He reasoned that maybe she never answered the phone at such odd hours, or maybe she was too deeply asleep to hear it.

Or maybe what he'd heard was her, screaming next door. Maybe she *couldn't* answer the phone. Galvanized by that thought, he threw on his clothes, holstered his gun and phone in his back pockets and sped to her house.

Banging on her door, he called to her. "Tomasina! It's me—Brogue—open up if you can!"

Hearing Brogue's voice, his fist pounding the front door, Tomasina yelled down from her bedroom, "I'm coming! Hold on!"

Breathless from her terrorist activity and startled to hear Brogue at the door, she tore off her clothes and put on her bathrobe.

"Tomasina!"

"I'm *coming*!"

She hurried down the stairs and opened the door.

He stood on the porch, chest heaving, his eyes making an anxious search of her face.

"You're okay?" he said.

She nodded. "Fine. Are you?"

He gave a half nod, as if not sure. "Sorry I got you up. Look, do you mind if I come in?" He held up both hands. "Not to hustle you anymore. No, ma'am."

"Why, then? You were angry when you left." She hated putting on an act, wished she hadn't had to take drastic measures.

"Right. I was pissed off, but this isn't about that. It's about something I think I heard over there." He cocked his head toward Kat's house.

"Oh, the ghost." She fixed a round-eyed, haunted look on her face. "Come in, come in."

He followed her to the living room, scoffing, "Ghost, schmost. I said I 'think' I heard something, Tomasina. I'm not sure it wasn't just a dream. I wondered if you heard anything. Dogs howling, maybe, or cats aggravating each other."

"What you heard sounds awful," she responded, hoping he wouldn't notice that she hadn't given him a direct answer. "It's been quiet here at my house, as far as I know."

He shrugged and took his gun and phone out of his back pockets in order to sit down. She stared at the gun, not having to force her eyes into saucer shapes this time, for she had never imagined him armed.

He explained, "I thought what I heard was you in trouble, so I came prepared. The safety's on. Don't worry about it."

Tomasina suppressed a sigh at the idea of him dashing over, armed and ready to protect and defend her. *What a hero. What a true blue knight.* At the same time, though, she felt a twinge of guilt.

"I'm sure it was all a dream now," he said. "I was having you—one, that is—right before I woke up."

She spoke quickly to discourage his conclusion. "Kat said she often heard sounds. She also felt icy cold spots in the air and saw vaporous mists floating around, as I told you before."

"I didn't see anything at all," he said, waving a hand in dismissal.

"But, considering what you heard tonight," she persisted, "shouldn't you reconsider buying the house?"

"My dream machine is what I heard," he said decisively. "That was all it could be."

"But, Brogue—"

He cut in, "Listen, your problem is you don't want me next door now that we've got history with each other. True?"

"True," she agreed, although it was only half true.

He went on, "You've clued me in on why you won't date cops. I've got the message, so we'll be nothing but neighbors from now on."

He got up, obviously ready to leave, and just as obviously ready to keep his option to buy Kat's house. Tomasina saw that it would be necessary to howl in the basement again after he went back to the house and before he went to sleep.

Beep-beep. His phone was ringing.

He answered it and Tomasina could tell by his expression and his rapid, cryptic responses that another homicide had been committed somewhere in San Francisco. "I'll be there in fifteen," he was saying.

He returned the phone and his gun to his back pockets. "Gotta hit the road."

She went with him to the door, struck by the helpless feeling that he might not return alive.

"Brogue." She covered her hand over his on the doorknob.

He glanced down at it and then sent a comprehending look into her eyes. "I'll keep safe, Tomasina," he said. "Don't worry about that."

"I can't help fearing the worst. Daddy and Keely..."

Brogue squared off with her, gripping her by the shoulders. "You listen to me, because I'll only say this once. The vibe I've got for you isn't just about getting you in bed. It's about caring more than I've cared in eight years. I don't know how it happened, but there it is. You say the word and I'll be back."

He released his grip, turned on his heel and strode out the door, shutting it firmly behind him.

Tomasina stood, stunned by the blunt force of the emotion he'd shown. She felt the unsteadying aftereffect of the almost violent hold he'd had on her shoulders. She had to back up and sit on the bottom step of the stairs.

Then she had to acknowledge that no involvement with Brogue might be out of the question for her now. It had been easier for her to push aside her enormous attraction to him when it had seemed that he only wanted her body.

But now Brogue's own acknowledgment of emotional attachment made it impossible to overlook her heart's response to him.

It was daunting to realize she'd been falling in love with him. Daunting to discover he'd been falling in love with her at the same time.

She had never felt so torn by her own emotions. She could say the word and risk loving a cop, or say nothing and keep safe. Either way, she was faced with the decision of a lifetime.

TOMASINA BEGAN the school week with one thing on her mind: Brogue. She hoped that letting some time pass without seeing him would diminish her feelings for him. Three days later, they were still as strong.

On Thursday, late in the afternoon, she and Casey Turner met at Spreckels Lake to relax and unwind by setting their model yachts out for a non-competitive spin.

Casey's *Painted Lady* was radio controlled like the *Xerxes Blue*, but whereas the *XB* was painted a shiny royal blue, the *PL*'s paint job was multicolored pastels. The two were a handsome pair, skimming companionably across the man-made lake in the light of the setting sun.

"Guess who I saw here yesterday afternoon at this same time," Casey said.

Tomasina radioed the *Xerxes* around a small flotilla of mallards. "Why do I have to guess?"

"It's more fun that way," Casey said, her plump cheeks creasing with a grin.

"Give me a hint, then."

"D-D-G-H."

"Easy. Since that's your favorite description of Mel Gibson, you must have been hallucinating yesterday afternoon."

"No, not Drop-Dead-Gorgeous-Heartthrob Mel this time," said Casey, who, they both knew, had bought the video of Gibson's *The Bounty* and viewed it twenty-seven times at last count.

"Casey, what other D-D-G-H do you know on sight?"

"Second hint," Casey said. She hummed this one in four instantly identifiable basso notes. "Dum-da-dum-dum."

"*Dragnet.*" Tomasina wrinkled her nose, pretending not to clue in. "You're switching from Mel to Jack Webb? Far short of D-D-G-H, if you ask me."

"Tomasina, get smart. C-O-P."

"Oh. You mean . . . ?"

"Yes, indeed. S.F.P.D. Right there on that bench across the lake, looking lonely for somebody I think I know. I was in the clubhouse, doing a few chores, so he didn't see me spot him."

Tomasina didn't know what to say. Brogue at the lake. Looking lonely.

Casey raised an eyebrow. "If I were you, I'd snatch him up. He certainly seemed interested at the car wash. And yesterday, you should have seen him glancing around as if he hoped with all his heart that you'd show up."

"It's more complicated than it might seem on the surface, Casey."

Casey clucked her tongue. "What a shame. Imagine the D-D-G babies you two could have together. Which reminds me, I heard from my own two gorgeous kids Sunday night."

Casey commenced with an update on the activities of her two sons in college, and Tomasina was glad for a change of subject.

The catch in her heart at the mere mention of Brogue was more evidence of how strongly she felt about him. The leap of her heart at Casey's comment about babies was even more proof. Would Brogue want a family if . . . ?

She quickly clipped that thought short.

THE NEXT DAY, Tomasina dressed in her hot-pink leo-tard and neon-yellow tights to do aerobics before breakfast. But before aerobics, she put on a long sweatshirt for warmth and went next door to make her morning check of Airwick, the garden and the house.

Entering the back gate, she was distressed to find that the house had been broken into through the rear door. The lock had been forced and the door was wide open. Alarmed, she ventured in and found that the house had been vandalized.

Tomasina rushed to her own house and called Brogue's work number. A cop, he'd know what to do from A to Z.

"He's not in his office yet this morning," the department switchboard operator informed her.

Tomasina declined to leave a message, then called his home number. He answered as if he were at his office.

"Homicide. Donovan."

"Brogue, it's me. Kat's house has been broken into and vandalized." She gave him brief facts.

"I'm on my way."

"Wait! Should I call the main police, too?"

"I'll take care of it. You stay out of the house until I get there. Are you teaching today?"

"No, Luke has the class."

"Stay put. I'm out the door."

Tomasina anxiously watched from her front porch for him. Within fifteen minutes, he pulled into the neighboring driveway. She ran down the steps and across the yard to his car. He was such a welcome sight she wished she could throw herself in his arms and give him a big, long kiss.

However, the expression on his face was closed and distant. She wasn't surprised by defensiveness; after all, she hadn't responded to his expression of affection.

He had no way of knowing she had intended to call him later today and say an encouraging word. But she couldn't explain that to him now.

She simply said what was topmost in her mind. "I'm glad you're here, Brogue."

An instant later, two uniformed officers—a man-and-woman team—arrived in a patrol car and got out. Brogue introduced both of them by their last names. The woman was McCafferty, the man Odenberg.

Tomasina took them all around to the rear door and they started scoping out the crime scene from that point. Moving inside the house, she pointed out the rest of the damage. The wall-to-wall carpets in two downstairs rooms had been stripped up and rolled back. Half the wainscoting in the dining room had been pried loose from the wallboards.

McCafferty went upstairs to check there, while Odenberg investigated the basement. Alone with Brogue, Tomasina contemplated the mess in the dining room.

"Not a typical vandalism scene," Brogue said. "No spray-paint graffiti, no smashed windows. I'd say somebody was looking for something in particular here. Something under the carpets, or in the walls. Was Kat Powell the type to squirrel away money and valuables all over the house?"

"No, she always had an active checking account at the bank. I remember her balancing her checkbook and reconciling the bank statements. She kept a bit of cash in the cookie jar, but that's all I recall."

"You know of anyone who'd think anything was hidden here?"

Tomasina shook her head. "Not a soul. Most of her financial resources went to environmental causes."

"Did you hear anyone over here last night?"

"No, but this has me worried about my own house now. I have an alarm system, but I suppose nothing is foolproof."

Brogue said, "Get a big dog food bowl with a name like Terminator or Jaws stenciled on it. Most burglars will pass up a house that might have the hound from hell inside."

McCafferty and Odenberg returned with nothing to report about the areas they'd inspected. "What's your take on this?" Brogue asked them. "Routine vandalism, or a break-in with a purpose?"

"Purpose," they both said, citing the same evidence as Brogue. Then they dispersed to go question the neighbors.

"I heard nothing over here last night," Tomasina told Brogue. She bit her lip and added, "I had trouble sleeping, but not because of any noise disturbance."

He nodded speculatively, his eyes narrowing intently on her. "Trouble sleeping," he repeated.

"Because of you, Brogue. I've missed you."

His eyes lit, but warily. "Yeah?"

"Yeah," she said, mimicking his tough, gritty tone. "Do you think we could have lunch together today, or will you be too busy combating crime?"

Smiling slightly now, he countered, "I'll take you out to breakfast, instead."

"All right." Her heart rose with anticipation. "I'll have to change clothes."

He shook his head, his eyes burning into hers. "Not for where I'm going to take you."

"Where?"

"My place."

"Sounds better than the Ritz," Tomasina murmured. And then she gave Brogue the big, long kiss she hadn't given him at first. She didn't end it until a moment before McCafferty and Odenberg came back in.

"You two wrap this up and do all the right stuff," Brogue ordered them. "Call a tech to dust for prints. Since this is almost my house, copy me on all reports. In the meantime, I've got a date to keep."

Tomasina got in the Porsche with him and fastened her seat belt. *Breakfast*, she was thinking, *in bed?*

10

BROGUE'S CONDO was as he had once described it to Tomasina: a basic rental unit. The rooms were small, the furniture functional, the floor plan a simple split-level.

"Not very romantic," he apologized as they went in, "but better than staying at your house today with two cops and a print tech next door. I don't want anybody gossiping about you."

Protective words, Tomasina thought, pleased by his concern for her reputation. He sounded a little possessive, too, in a nice way, which pleased her more. She was having her own proprietary feelings about him, as well.

"Brogue, what if you get one of those calls while we're here?"

"I'm going to make sure I won't," he said, picking up the phone.

Tomasina looked into the aquarium in his living room while he phoned the department. She counted ten neon tetras in the tank. Their iridescent markings flashed and swirled in the clear water.

Finished with the phone, Brogue came up behind her and splayed his hands over the lower front of her sweatshirt.

"So," he said, nuzzling the side of k, "you
missed me. Couldn't sleep well without t else?"

She replied, "I kept thinking of what I feel
the same way about you, Brogue. I've tions
in the past, but this is different."

"Not just because I'm a cop?"

"That's part of it, yet the difference is
that."

"Vibes," he whispered in her ear.

"Yes." She used one of his recurring
"Out-of-this-world vibes."

"Do you want breakfast yet, or somet

"Something else, please."

His hands slid to the hem of her sweatsh
up under it, beneath the weighted curves o bed
She leaned back against his broad chest an
eyes as his fingers fanned higher, over the tl
ric she was wearing.

"I've imagined you like this a million ti
sina. In hot pink. All mine. Lift your arms.

She complied and he slipped the sweatshir
head. Still behind her, he traced his fingertips a
scooped neckline of her leotard. He stopped at t
ter and dipped one finger into the deep cleavag
tween her breasts.

"I want you," she said with a sigh. "All day."

She felt him smile against her skin, and lightly scrap
his teeth down the curve of her neck to the top of her
shoulder. "You've got me," he replied. "No interrup-
tions."

his hands with hers, Tomasina led them to
her breasts. Then she raised her hands and
fingers behind his neck, a motion that drove
Apples up into the centers of his palms.

her head, she lifted her lips to his and shared
ply tender, yet ravenous kiss that stole her
nd fired her blood. Brogue hardened behind
erection boldly nudging the base of her spine.
hand smoothed down from her breasts to cup
und. His fingers rubbed gently, finding the soft
She felt her thighs tremble, her knees weaken.
ogue, carry me to bed. Make love with me at

lifted her up in his arms and took her there. His
was unmade, the bedclothes rumpled.
I wasn't expecting you," he quipped huskily, set-
g her in the center of it and kneeling over her.

She gave him a slow smile and let her gaze slide from
is face to the strained fly of his trousers. "You're ex-
ecting me now, Brogue."

He leaned over and took a condom from his bed-
stand drawer. Tomasina opened the package so there
would be no delay later.

They undressed each other on the bed, delighting in
every inch of exposed skin, tossing clothes every-
where. Soon, bare of everything, they lay together,
embraced and entwined, excited and exuberant with
discovery and desire.

Brogue, fascinated with her breasts, kissed them and
sucked the tips and nuzzled his face in the soft between. He murmured dark, sexy, incoherent words

against her skin as she rubbed circles over his chest and nipples.

He moved his mouth down to her tummy and kept hot little kisses sizzling all the way to the junction of her thighs. Her fingers wove through his dark hair as she opened without question to him, inviting the exploration he sought.

"Brogue, yes," she gasped.

"Here?" he murmured to her as his tongue found her tender bud.

"Yes . . ." Her hips lifted to his gently laving, sucking kiss. It brought soft, breathy cries from her. "Oh, Brogue . . . you're wonderful!"

"So are you, Tomasina."

"Brogue." She trembled and writhed when his tongue glided into her and swirled. "Don't make me . . . not yet . . . not yet . . ."

It was almost too much, but not quite, because Brogue showed a masterful gift for sensing her crest as she approached it. Easing away, he kissed her inner thighs, then returned again to her center.

Tomasina had never been aroused so well—never so sensually, intuitively, lovingly well. Could she ever let Brogue Donovan go after this?

He rose to his knees, powerfully aroused and clearly at his own limit, gazing down at her body. She kissed her fingers and let them carry the kiss to his throbbing tip.

"Not this time," he replied to the intimate question her gesture had posed.

She took up the condom. He breathed deep for control as she covered him. Then he stretched over her and kissed her mouth as he entered her. She rose to him, twined her legs high around him and met his long, deep thrusts.

Hands planted above her shoulders, he drew his head away from hers and looked into her eyes as he moved inside her.

"All mine," he murmured possessively.

"All day," she rejoined in the same tone.

She recognized the urgent sexual need in his gaze, and she saw something else, as well. She saw the warm light of spring in his eyes where there had been winter earlier.

It was her last thought before she came to a rolling, soaring climax. She felt him shudder as she cried out his name at the very height of her ecstasy. His rhythm raced out of control then, fast and wild, as he found his own exploding, shattering release.

Peaceful and utterly contented afterward, Tomasina drowsed in the embrace of her true blue knight and fell into blissful sleep with him.

KAT, DEREK AND SAMANTHA were aghast to see police in their haunt when they returned to it after an overnight visit to Sausalito, north of the city. Their adventurous outing had been Derek's idea.

But now they all wished they had never taken a night's break from the house. "The wainscoting!" Kat exclaimed. "The carpets, the broken back door!"

They all looked at one another and shared a shocking thought, *Rival ghosts?*

"No," said Derek, after a quick inspection. "This was earthly work. See the crowbar marks on the damaged walls."

Sam immediately zoomed next door to check on her niece. Returning a moment later, she reported worriedly, "Tomasina isn't home, but her car is there. She's missing."

"Now, now," Sam soothed. "Tomasina often takes the buses and streetcars here and there. She may have gone where parking is a problem."

They turned to eavesdrop on what the male police officer was saying to the fingerprint technician out of the female officer's hearing.

"Donovan looked whipped like you wouldn't believe. Then he took off in his Porsche with the blonde from next door." The cop drew an hourglass shape in the air with his hands and let out a low whistle.

"A dream babe, eh?" the tech said.

The cop panted for effect. "Marilyn Monroe all over again."

"So there," Kat said to Sam. "Tomasina is with Brogue. Perhaps this is their big day to—" she paused for a roguish wink "—get on with it."

Sam was calmed, but not for long. "Who on earth wreaked this awful damage? We've got a true mystery on our hands now. How on earth will we ever solve it?"

TOMASINA AND BROGUE didn't eat breakfast until early evening, and then only after they had exhausted themselves in bed all day. They showered together, then dressed and went to a nearby diner for some casual, but hearty, fare.

There, over corned-beef hash and eggs, Tomasina made a difficult confession to Brogue. She took his hand in hers over the dinner table and drew a deep breath.

"Brogue, I have something to tell you. It may make you angry, but it has to be said. Now rather than later."

His fingers tightened on hers. "What?"

"I—I've sort of been deceiving you. Not lying, exactly, not as your ex-wife did. Try to keep an open mind while I explain. It's all about Kat's garden."

Slowly, haltingly, she began telling him of her promise to Kat, about the Flying Flowers Society and the butterflies, about Primo, the perfume oil, the dry ice and Airwick. She was getting near the part about finding the tunnel, when Brogue stopped her.

"Maybe you didn't outright lie to me," he said, "but you manipulated me."

She protested, "But I didn't succeed. In fact, I can't explain to myself or you why the lights smelled like carnations that night, or why the dry ice didn't produce cold spots. The rolling sound couldn't have been Airwick, who was high up in the attic crawl space."

"Just the same," he countered, "you were doing your level best to thwart me, and I didn't have a clue."

Keeping a grip on his hand, even though he was trying to pull away, she said, "You didn't suffer any loss from what I did."

"I'm suffering a loss of some trust right now, Tomasina."

She insisted, "I'm telling you the truth and coming clean so that you *won't* distrust me. How can you distrust the facts?"

"Easy. You weren't truthful until now. I see where this is leading, too. You want me to change my mind about the backyard."

She nodded. "Yes, I do. My yacht, the *Xerxes Blue*, is named after a local butterfly species that is extinct now. Kat and I worked together to breed and reintroduce the green hairstreak species, which is becoming quite rare."

Brogue was shaking his head. "You're an impossible dreamer. I knew it all along."

"And you're a cynic," she argued gently. "Butterflies are like pieces of a dream made real. If you would learn just a little about them, they might inspire you with hope for their survival."

Brogue sighed, appearing less angry, but more resolute than ever. "I've got my own dream for that house, Tomasina. I'm not about to waste a big yard on weeds and mud puddles and gnarly old fruit trees. Forget talking me out of it."

She could see there'd be no use in telling him about the tunnel. What would it matter anyway, since it would remain a secret? He'd never have to know.

"Brogue, don't let this come between us before you give some thought to what I've said so far."

He gave her a long, uncertain look. "How do I know I can trust anything you say now?"

"How do you know you can't?" She stroked his fingers, which were relaxing, and smiled into his eyes. "I loved what we had together today and that's the absolute truth from the bottom of my heart."

"Yeah?" His expression was changing.

"Yeah, tough guy. I want more of what we had, too."

He laced his fingers with hers and said, "God, it was heaven on earth. We both agree on that, at least."

"Take me back to your bed, Brogue."

He didn't argue with that.

ON MONDAY AT SCHOOL, Tomasina accidentally found a delightful way to win time for the garden. It presented itself during the class's weekly show-and-tell hour. The theme this time was "Something Interesting I Did over the Weekend."

One student, Katie, brought a poster from the circus she'd gone to with her family on Sunday afternoon. Another, Jonathan, brought shells from an oyster farm he'd visited. Sandra, the last student to speak, brought a little birdhouse she had made from a plastic soft-drink bottle.

Sandra had painted flowers and butterflies on it, and as she carried it to the front of the room for her speech, Katie exclaimed, "A butterfly house! Let's make some in crafts class."

Katie's words were Tomasina's inspiration. The class had visited Kat's garden last autumn to learn about it. Two of Tomasina's green hairstreak chrysalises were in the classroom, and the children had been watching for the butterflies to emerge. So, after Sandra finished,

Tomasina remarked on Katie's bright idea and casually reminded the class about the garden.

Katie, bless her round little freckled face, said just what Tomasina was hoping to hear. "Miss Walden, could we make the houses to put in the garden? For the butterflies to live in after they pop out?"

Tomasina turned the question to the class. "What does everybody else think?"

They went wild with enthusiasm.

She cautioned, "One thing we'll have to do first is make a telephone call to someone we all know."

"Who?" they wanted to know.

She told them, explained why the call was necessary and asked if anybody in the class would like to make it.

"Me, me, me," clamored Katie. "It was *my* idea."

BROGUE NEVER GOT calls from kids, so he was more than surprised when a kid phoned his office number on Monday at ten o'clock.

"This is who?" he queried after the caller identified herself in a small, tentative voice.

"Katie Prentiss. From Serra Vista Elementary School."

Serra Vista, he thought. *Tomasina's school.*

"Okay, Katie Prentiss. What can I do for you?"

"Can we put some houses in your garden? For butterflies?"

Houses for what?

"Katie, are you a third-grader at Serra Vista?"

"Yes! How do you know?"

Brogue closed his eyes. He knew, he knew. The clues were falling into place.

"I know Miss Walden, Katie." *A little too well now.*

"So can we?" Katie inquired. "They need houses to live. Come to school and see."

"Who thought up the idea of these houses, Katie?"

"Me, so I got to call and ask. Can we?"

"Sure, sure you can." He wasn't going to shoot down that sweet, pleading voice.

"Yeah! Thank you, Mr. Lieutenant!"

"Katie, would you put Miss Walden on the phone now? I'd really like to talk to her."

A moment later, Tomasina came on the line. "Hello, Lieutenant. We all thank you so much. The green hairstreaks thank you, too."

"Tomasina, you put those kids up to this, didn't you?"

"Lieutenant, the students will tell you it was Katie's idea from A to Z. As Katie said a moment ago, come to school and see for yourself."

"I'll bet they all want to thank me personally," he growled.

"Of course they do. You're one of the good guys, as Jonathan Raines so perfectly described you when I told the class why we'd need your permission."

"This isn't going to change my mind about the backyard," he warned.

"We'll start making the houses tomorrow afternoon during crafts hour from one to two o'clock, Lieutenant. Please come to school then, if you can."

He was incredulous at how blithe she sounded. "Have you seen my caseload?"

"No," she replied softly, "but you should see my happy class. Many thanks again, Lieutenant. Goodbye."

ONE OF THE GOOD GUYS, but with a bad attitude, Brogue grudgingly went to school Tuesday afternoon. He wore his uniform, too, because it stood for so much with small kids. And maybe also because he suspected it rang Tomasina's female chimes.

He didn't mind keeping her turned on, even though she was actively conspiring against him about the backyard. He was giving her the benefit of the doubt about whose idea the butterfly houses were. Anyway, he couldn't stay away from her now that he'd had a taste of heaven on earth.

He wasn't blinded by love, but he couldn't deny how nearsighted he'd started getting about some things.

She'll come around about the yard, he kept telling himself. She'll come around.

"Oh, look who's here," she enthused when he walked into the classroom. "Our hero, Lieutenant Donovan."

"Hello, Miss Walden." He gave the students a wave. "Hi, third grade."

He noted that Tomasina had her blue sweater-dress on. Her own way of keeping *him* turned on? It was doing a damn good job.

The kids crowded around him, some of them awed by him, others jumping up and down with excitement. Tomasina pointed out red-haired, freckle-nosed Katie.

It was all enough to make a homicide cop forget about drive-by murders and morgues for a while.

"So," he said to them, "where are these houses you're making?"

They took him to a big worktable at the back of the classroom and showed him what they were creating out of plastic soft-drink bottles and colorful paints.

Katie Prentiss wanted to know, "How many butterflies are going to live in your garden?"

At a loss, Brogue had to question Tomasina with a quick glance.

"Two hundred," she said.

He blinked at her and she affirmed that yes, he had heard right.

"We've gotta make lots of houses," one boy said.

Brogue visualized two hundred painted plastic thingamabobs hanging all over the weeds and thistles and twisted tree limbs in his backyard. Not to mention a tame, unscented skunk wandering around out there.

He cleared his throat. "They don't each need a house, do they?"

Several kids said yes. Tomasina didn't say anything, he noticed. Her beautiful brown eyes were dancing with amusement.

He asked another pertinent question. "How long do these houses have to hang around?"

"Till the end of school," said Katie.

June, Brogue thought with an inner wince.

The next thing he knew, one of the kids put a picture book, *Flying Flowers,* in front of his face. Another student came running up with a pint jar that had something brown and dead-looking in it. He got a ten-minute crash course in metamorphosis.

Tomasina finally spoke up. "We'll have a short field trip to hang the houses in the garden when they're finished. If that's okay with you, Lieutenant."

Twenty-four innocent, cherubic little faces turned up to him for his reply.

"Sure." He gave them all a heroic, helpless smile. "Okay."

11

TOMASINA WENT to bed late Tuesday night not sure whether she and Brogue were still friends and lovers. His expression had been impossible to read when he'd left her classroom earlier that day.

After saying a little prayer for him to understand, she settled down for the night. She was almost asleep when a strange feeling came over her. A prickly sensation that something wasn't quite right next door. Had she heard a sound from over there? She couldn't be certain.

Becoming increasingly unsettled, yet not able to identify why, she got out of bed and peered at Kat's house through the curtains. Everything looked calm next door, except that the front porch light and a light she'd left on in the kitchen had both apparently gone out. New bulbs, they should still be burning.

She frowned, knowing she wouldn't go to sleep now unless she made a quick check to be sure all was well. She'd just go see, and change the bulbs.

Dressed a few minutes later in jeans and a pullover, she took two new light bulbs with her and went next door. Entering through the front door, she flipped the inside light switch. Nothing happened.

Then, hearing low, creaky noises, she tiptoed to the open door of the dining room, where they seemed to be coming from. She heard sounds of wood being pried away from the wall.

The vandal again? Or could it be a ghost?

Tomasina stood still, her heart pounding. She swallowed hard, rooted to the spot. She knew she should turn and go, call the police, but her feet wouldn't move.

There was the sensation of an invisible force gently pushing at her, like a hand against her chest, as if she were being urged to run out the front door.

She froze as she heard the prying sound stop. There came a guttural, unintelligible curse from the dining room. Then a dark shape loomed in the doorway.

It so frightened her that she dropped the light bulbs. They shattered on the floor. The shape made a throaty sound of startled surprise, sudden awareness, and grabbed her. She screamed, flailed her fists against it, feeling the textures of heavy cloth and knit wool against her knuckles.

A human being, she thought as she struggled to break free. *A man.* He had something in one hand—something metal and heavy. He raised it above her head.

"Stop!" she screamed, trying to dodge it. It came down on her shoulder and glanced off. Up it went again. "No!"

There was a dull thud as it hit down on the side of her skull. She sagged to the floor. Colors exploded behind her eyes and she writhed in agonizing pain on the splintered glass of the light bulbs.

From a great distance it seemed, she heard feet crunching over the glass, running out the front door, down the steps and away.

Moaning, blinded by pain, she struggled to her knees and then to her feet. She staggered to the doorway, then to the porch, fighting for breath and balance.

She had to get home. Stumbling and lurching, falling at times and righting herself, she gritted her teeth and reached her own porch. Finally inside, she fell again and had to crawl to the telephone in the kitchen.

Near the end of her strength, she called 911 for emergency aid. Someone answered and Tomasina could only get out her street address and a broken plea. "Help . . . help me . . ." The receiver slipped from her hand.

BROGUE SAT next to Tomasina's hospital bed, holding her hand, praying for her to regain consciousness. The doctors had said she would—in time.

"Tomasina?" He'd been repeating her name for two hours with no response from her. "Tomasina?"

His heart skipped as her eyelids fluttered for the first time. Her lips moved and she turned her head slightly to the sound of his voice. He touched her cheek and her hair, murmuring her name again.

Her lips parted and a tiny whisper emerged. "Brogue?"

"I'm here. Right here." Brogue heard his voice shake with emotion.

She smiled slightly and her eyes fluttered open. They slowly focused on his face. Another whisper emerged, stronger this time. "Hi, Brogue."

"Hi, sleeping beauty." He leaned forward and gently kissed her lips. "In case you're wondering, you're in the emergency hospital."

"Yes, I see." Her whisper strengthened to a soft murmur. "How did you find out?"

"McCafferty was on patrol and heard the aid call go over the radio. She thought I'd be interested. She was damned right, too."

"I hurt," Tomasina said with a sigh.

Brogue clasped her hand in his, hating his helplessness. "You've got a concussion and some minor cuts from broken glass. You've been here about two hours."

"Can I go home?"

"That depends on what the medics say." He pushed the nursing call button. "They need to know you're conscious, and do a few tests. After that, I've got questions about what happened, when you feel up to answering them."

She nodded gingerly. "I remember everything, I think. Except I don't know who hit me."

"We'll find out," he assured her, giving her another soft kiss. "In the meantime, I'm here with you until you get released."

"Brogue, I'm so glad you are."

"Nothing could keep me away, Tomasina."

She quirked an emotional smile at him. "Not even two hundred butterfly houses?"

"For the time being," he replied gruffly, "no."

THE NEXT DAY at noon, Brogue took Tomasina home. She had medical orders to rest in bed for two days and not work for the rest of the week.

"I'll stay with you today and overnight," Brogue said, carrying her up to her bedroom, "and maybe tomorrow, too, if I can."

He put her to bed and made lunch for her. She called her mother later in the afternoon and told her what had happened.

Gwen was audibly appalled and upset. "I'll pack a suitcase and catch the next flight to see you," she said.

"Mom, that's not necessary because Brogue is watching over me."

"Brogue, the deep voice who picked up your phone the other morning?"

"Yes. However, if you could come earlier than you had originally planned to visit, that would help."

"I'll change my plane ticket to the day after tomorrow," Gwen said a little more calmly. "Friday."

"Perfect."

Gwen's voice turned thoughtful—and curious. "Since Brogue will have his eye on you until I arrive, it must mean more than you let on that morning."

"I'm not sure what it means, Mom. I didn't tell you he's a homicide detective—a lieutenant, no less. In fact, he's next door right now, unofficially investigating the incident."

"Ah." Her mother had a silent moment. "That's why you sound so uncertain about him."

Tomasina warned, "Don't get your hopes up, okay?"

"I understand, honey. I'll call later with my flight schedule. You do every little thing the doctors say until I get there."

"I will. I promise. Bye."

Tomasina hung up the phone and heard Brogue come in the front door a few minutes later. She could tell he was tiptoeing, trying to be quiet and not disturb her.

"I'm awake," she called to him from her room. "Come up."

He came to her, taking off his bomber jacket, shaking raindrops from it. "It's sprinkling out there," he said as he hung it on the doorknob. "The forecast says another big storm's brewing."

She smiled at him from the bed. "You know where the flashlights and candles are if the electricity blinks out tonight."

He moved the phone from her bed to the nightstand, then kicked off his shoes and lay on his side next to her. Propped up on one elbow, he contemplated her face with quiet concern in his eyes.

"How are you doing?"

"Mom's coming day after tomorrow. I told her about you."

"I'll meet her plane at the airport," Brogue offered, "so she won't have to take a cab."

Tomasina sighed gratefully. "What would I do without you right now? You've notified the school, kept my name and address out of the newspaper report, made me soup for lunch and practically spoon-fed it to me."

He said, "You leave everything to me, beautiful. Just rest and get well and don't worry about anything else."

"What did you find out next door, Brogue?"

"Not much. More wainscoting torn up." He took a tiny plastic bag from his front shirt pocket. "Odenberg found this in the broken glass. A stud earring. Not yours, since your ears aren't pierced. Maybe Kat Powell's, maybe not."

Tomasina examined it through the plastic. A small gold sunburst. "I know someone who wears earrings like this. Primo's nephew-in-law."

"Primo, the magician you told me about at the diner?"

Tomasina told him as much as she knew about Rick Solari, his shady past of vandalism and drug use, and also about Rick delivering the dry ice.

Brogue was sitting up straight when she finished. "We may have our assailant if he's missing an earring. Not that we could pin anything on him with just this for evidence. If he left prints, we'll nail him."

"I wish I had actually seen who it was," Tomasina said. "It was too dark. I only felt him. He was about Rick's height, though."

She had already described to Brogue her other impressions of the vandal, which hadn't provided a physical description.

"His motive must be that he thinks valuables are boarded up in the house," Brogue mused. "Where would he get that idea?"

"Brogue, he mentioned reading a diary that Primo has. Derek Powell's diary. Kat's soldier-of-fortune brother."

She explained that Derek and Primo had become fast friends in Italy, and that Derek and Kat had sponsored Primo's immigration and citizenship.

"Why does Primo have his diary?" Brogue asked.

"They were close friends," she said. "Kat passed it on to him after Derek died."

"When did he die?"

"Seven years ago, a year before Aunt Sam. He had two strokes, the first one a month before his death and then one that was fatal. Ironically, his wife died two weeks after him."

"What do you mean 'ironically'?"

She told Brogue about Aunt Sam and Derek. "Their affair spanned thirty years," she added wistfully, "and they kept it a secret the whole time. My aunt shared it with me just before her own death. Poor Aunt Sam."

"You once said Derek told tales of hidden treasure," Brogue recalled. "Was there any truth to them?"

"I suppose there could have been, but he didn't live a wealthy life. He stayed with Kat in the times between his trips here and there. I think he was more of a restless adventurer than a soldier of fortune, but he did love to talk, and told fascinating stories—especially about diamond mines in South America."

"Maybe he told the same tales in his diary," Brogue said. "Rick reads it, gets ideas, starts tearing up the house. I'll bet he's missing this little earring today, unless he's got a spare."

Tomasina said, "He wore so many. Several suns like that one on one ear, and also a few nose rings."

"Can you recall how many suns?"

She thought for a moment. "Seven. I remember thinking it was a lucky number."

"He could have killed you," Brogue said in a low, ferocious tone.

She nodded, and winced when she felt pain shoot to her head and shoulder. "Luckily he didn't. If I hadn't gone over there in the middle of the night, it would never have happened."

"Don't blame yourself. You were in the wrong place at the wrong time, granted, but that's not the issue. Bodily harm is the issue."

"I'll be more careful from now on," she promised.

"I need to make some phone calls about all this downstairs," Brogue said, standing up and unplugging her phone so she wouldn't be disturbed if it rang. "Close your eyes and rest. Need anything before I go?"

She nodded, even though it hurt again. "A kiss."

Brogue knelt beside the bed and gave her a tender, adoring kiss on the lips.

"I love you, Tomasina," he said with grave certainty.

"And I love you," she rejoined softly, "my true blue knight."

He left the room, then she closed her eyes and drifted off to sleep.

BROGUE MADE SEVERAL CALLS from the kitchen phone. He requested a background check and fingerprint ID on Rick Solari, among other things. The information transfer from New York to San Francisco would take some time.

He dialed Maggissimo and asked for Rick.

"Speaking," said the young nasal voice that answered.

Assured that Rick was there in the shop, Brogue hung up. He got hold of a North Beach beat cop and asked him to drop by the magic shop on the double.

"I need a count and ID of the clerk's sun-shaped ear studs," he said.

"Old Primo's wife's bad-news nephew?" the beat cop asked.

"Bingo. You're familiar with him?"

"I've seen him skulking around. Didn't count his ear studs, though. What's he done that I missed?"

"It's hard to say for sure," Brogue replied. "Call me when you've got a count." He gave Tomasina's number and signed off.

Then he phoned several jewelry stores to determine if sunburst stud earrings were common stock in the city. Discouragingly, it turned out that they were all the rage this year. Over half the stores he polled had more than one style of sunburst stud. There was one that had fifteen variations.

Since the phone was on the wall where Tomasina's butterfly jars were shelved, Brogue had a close-up view of them. He gazed into several of them while waiting for North Beach to call back with the earring count.

Knowing the jars hadn't been on the shelves the night he'd had dinner here, Brogue reflected that Tomasina had been extremely good at hiding things from him before she confessed her deceit.

He still had a sore spot about that, but it was healing. The balm was in knowing she'd been deceptive for understandable reasons. Her effort to save a garden was one reason, and he could see that Tomasina had also been trying to curtail her own attraction to him.

He couldn't really fault her for wanting to shield herself from heartbreak. He'd been doing the same thing himself, in his own way, for eight years.

His old motto—Don't Park Your Heart Here—no longer applied. Now he was in love and it was making him rethink everything. The phone rang, startling him. He picked it up in midring.

"Donovan."

"Seven pierced studs on the bad-news boy," said his North Beach connection. "All identical, all on one ear. Plain, gold tone, three-sixteenths of an inch diameter."

Brogue cursed. "He must have a spare, then."

"What?"

"Never mind."

"He's got three schnozz rings, too, if you're interested."

"Not. Thanks for your trouble, and keep an eye out around there for him. Anything suspicious, I'd like to know."

Hanging up the phone, Brogue growled in frustration. His stomach started to do its usual routine of knotting up. He glanced at one of the jars and saw a movement in it. A quiver. As he watched, it did it again.

It was like a heart beginning to pulse with life. Like his own heart, he realized. Coming alive to love again, little by little and beat by beat.

Thinking about Tomasina, and his growing love for her, helped ease his inner tension. She had brought humor and happiness into his life. She had revived his hope that good might triumph over evil in the end. All because of an impossible dreamer, a dreamer he had almost lost.

Solari, he thought, his hand forming a fist. *You're not going to get away with it. Not with me on your case.*

12

TOMASINA AWOKE in the early evening, much stronger and feeling less pain. Brogue made dinner and brought it to her on a tray—a simple meal of eggs, toast and tea. One item, to her surprise, was not something to eat. It was a butterfly jar.

"Something's going on in there," Brogue told her as he arranged her scarlet pillows around her for comfort. "I figured you'd want to have a look."

Delighted, she said, "It's an early bird. There are always a few that get a jump on the others."

As she ate, more quivering took place in the jar. She explained to Brogue that the top of the chrysalis had split and that soon the butterfly would emerge, headfirst, and pull itself up out of the case.

Brogue gave her an apprehensive look. "Am I going to have to butterfly-sit tonight?"

"No, but I've done that at times. Kat once kept a batch in her bedroom for two months because the weather was so cold that year. They slept at night in an empty fish aquarium about the size of yours."

"Fascinating," Brogue said, his tone implying something considerably less.

However, Tomasina detected a flicker of interest in his eyes. She hoped it was challenging his plan for Kat's garden. Deciding not to press for too much at one time, she changed her tune.

"You make delicious scrambled eggs, Brogue."

He chuckled. "You haven't seen the mess I made making them."

He went on to tell her what he'd found out by phone while she'd been asleep. She listened with a sinking feeling that the crime would go unsolved. Suspecting Rick was one thing, proving anything against him was another.

"Fingerprints may be the only hope at this point, but he probably wasn't stupid enough to go over there barehanded," Brogue said.

Tomasina reasoned, "For hidden treasure, imagined or real, wouldn't he be tempted to return soon?"

"Maybe. Depends on how greedy—or desperate—he is for whatever he's seeking. As soon as I move into the house, he'll have to get through me and the security system I want to have installed. His time is limited, and maybe he knows it."

"You're going to buy the house, then," she concluded.

He replied, "I've got to, before the option expires." His voice lowered. "You're still not happy about it, are you?"

"Not about the garden," she replied with a glance at the chrysalis.

"Tomasina, your third-graders have my hands tied until June. Isn't that enough?"

"Butterflies need a year-round habitat," she tried to say as gently as possible, while still holding her firm position. "They have several stages of life and the garden is a primary food source. It's also necessary for courting and mating, as well as basking and puddling."

"Puddling?" He looked dubious. "Come again?"

"The sodium from mud puddles helps the males mate. It's sex fuel."

Brogue got a gleam in his eyes. "Finally, something *I* can relate to."

"You'll never look at puddles the same way again," she taunted with a provocative smile. "If I catch you sipping from one, I'll know what you're after."

"I'm always fueled up for you, Tomasina."

"Even now," she questioned uncertainly, "when I'm all cut up and stuck in bed?"

He nodded. "You turn me on, no matter what or when. Yesterday, today, tomorrow."

"I feel the same about you. I've got a mild concussion, but I'm not brain-dead and I keep thinking about making love with you—like right now."

Brogue set the tray aside and lay down next to her on the bed. Gently and very carefully, he eased his arms around her and held her.

"I don't want you to think I can't wait to make love again," he murmured, lying still with her. "I can wait as long as it takes for you to get well."

He brushed his fingers tenderly over the soft fabric of her nightshirt at her breasts. He kissed her eyelids and her lips.

"I feel so much better when you're close to me," she whispered. "You're better for me than bed rest. Let's make love without intercourse."

Brogue said, "God, I'm dying for anything you want, but I also don't want to hurt you."

"Brogue, not sharing with you would hurt me more. Slip off your clothes . . . please."

He did, slowly, while she just as slowly unbuttoned the front of her nightshirt all the way down. Then they lay together, touching and caressing, kissing and sighing. His hand slipped between her thighs and her hand curled around his hard shaft. He stroked her and she stroked him, on and on with gentle movements and subtle rhythms, drawing out the pleasure and emotion, building to the peak, degree by degree.

Loving and sharing, each to each and one to one, they came to the joy of mutual surrender.

Later, much later, Tomasina roused from peaceful sleep and found Brogue beside her, gazing into the jar he had brought on the dinner tray.

"Look," he murmured.

She did, and saw that a fragile, living thing had emerged into being. A precious, lovely butterfly.

GWEN WALDEN ARRIVED in San Francisco on a midday flight from Los Angeles. As Brogue had offered, he met her at the airport and drove her home to Tomasina, who had progressed from bed rest to being quietly up and around the house.

Tomasina opened the front door and waved as they arrived in Brogue's Porsche. When they emerged from the car, she immediately saw that Gwen liked Brogue and that the feeling was mutual. Brogue couldn't stay, though; homicide was calling him after two days off, and he also needed to check out the Rick Solari information from New York.

"I'll stop by this evening sometime," he promised, and then left again.

"Lieutenant Brogue Donovan is exactly what I expected from his voice when I called that morning," Gwen said as she unpacked her suitcase in the guest room.

Tomasina sat in one of the rocking chairs, smiling with love for her slim, pretty mother. Gwen's blond hair was frosted with gray and her creamy skin was clear, smoother than one would expect for a woman in her midfifties. She had verve and vitality, and maintained a satisfying job as a free-lance paralegal.

"I don't know what to do about him," Tomasina confided.

"He appears to be in love, and so do you, Tomasina. There is usually only one thing to do about that."

Tomasina said, "You're going to take your words back when you hear that he's buying Kat's house."

"I already know. He told me in the car."

"Did he say he's going to tear out the garden to put in a swimming pool and sports court?"

Her mother abruptly stopped unpacking and came to sit down in the other rocking chair. "He didn't mention that, and I'm afraid I can see why."

"That's his plan, Mom."

"It isn't the only thing that gives you doubts, though, is it?"

Tomasina shook her head. "I can't believe I've fallen in love with a police officer. I did my best not to get involved. Each time he leaves for work, I fear that he'll never, ever return."

"I saw your worried expression when he drove away," her mother said with an understanding nod. "You know, he told me on the way here from the airport about being shot several years ago. It came into the conversation naturally because I brought up Reece and Keely first."

"A third tragedy would just tear me apart, Mom."

"Honey, you can't ignore that Brogue stands out among the men you've known. The others—nice as they've been—never captured your heart. It was never right, and now somehow it is."

"You've known him all of one hour," Tomasina argued. "How can you be so sure he's right for me?"

Gwen sighed, smiling. "Simply because I knew you before you knew yourself. You won't understand that inner knowing until you have children of your own."

She rose and continued unpacking. Tomasina rocked in the chair and pictured children of her own.

"I'm so glad you're here, Mom."

"I am, too, honey. Your being attacked is more than I can stand to think about. Knowing you were in Brogue's care has been a saving grace."

"It's been one for me, as well," Tomasina murmured.

"Honey, do you remember Samantha saying it's best to love and lose than not to love at all?"

"No, I don't think so."

"Maybe she only said it to me, then, after we lost Reece and Keely. My grief was so crushing each time, and I felt she was wrong. Over the years, though, I've come to see the wisdom of her words. Pondering them might help you see your way with Brogue."

The phone rang and Gwen answered it.

"Primo!" Tomasina heard her exclaim. "*Ciao* to you, too...oh, you did...much better...please do...we'll love seeing you . . . okay, *ciao*."

Tomasina had instructions from Brogue not to say anything to anyone about Stella's nephew and his suspected role in the assault and vandalism. So she kept mum about it when Gwen came back into the guest room.

"The Maggios want to drop in for a few minutes tonight with a get-well bouquet for you."

"That's kind of them. I wonder how they knew I wasn't feeling well."

"Stella heard it at church from Casey."

"Oh, that's right. Same church."

"Well," said Gwen, "since it's noon, I'll make lunch. You'll sit and watch."

Tomasina started to chuckle. "When we get to the kitchen, don't be surprised by the mess. Brogue can cook, but not without major consequences."

Laughing, Tomasina and Gwen went down the stairs together.

PRIMO ARRIVED after dinnertime that evening with magic tricks up his sleeves, Stella on his arm, and his nephew-in-law grudgingly in tow.

Tomasina was appalled to see Rick slink into her living room. But for a multitude of reasons, she tried not to show it beyond the initial shock. There was Brogue's dictum not to speak of the suspect. There was her respect for old friends, the Maggios, who knew nothing of Rick's skulduggery.

As well, it was apparent that Rick didn't know he'd been circumstantially incriminated. Finally, there was Brogue's call late that afternoon advising that none of the fingerprints from the house matched Rick's prints from New York.

No accusations could be made against Rick without evidence. Interrogating him without reason was out of the question, too.

Now Rick Solari was slumped in a chair, looking bored beyond words by the visit his aunt had apparently dragged him to. Tomasina knew that Primo would never have brought him along otherwise.

However, Primo was making the best of a bad situation with sleight-of-hand card and coin tricks. Gwen graciously served coffee and cake. Stella perched on the edge of the sofa, adoring every move that Primo made.

And Tomasina had to act ignorant of the truth about Rick.

He lit a cigarette, announcing, "If anybody minds my smoke, too bad."

"I mind this smoke," Primo vigorously protested. "You do not own *cara*'s house, Mr. No Respect."

Timid Stella showed a faint spark. "Ricky, the smoke is not good for Uncle Primo's angina. Be a good boy, *per favore*, for Auntie."

Rick, of course, smoked on and blew chains of smoke rings into the air.

Tomasina caught a who-is-this-jerk glance from Gwen. *Mom, if only you knew,* she thought.

Rick was eyeing Gwen through the smoke. "You're Samantha's baby sister?" he questioned. "Samantha who used to live here?"

"Yes," Gwen replied. "She was many years older than I. Why do you ask?"

"Just curious," Rick replied with a shrug. "I've read about her in Unc's old book. Until Unc hid it, that is."

All eyes turned to Primo, who waved a hand dismissively and said, "Not a book. It is only Derek's diary. Many big fictions Derek wrote, and tiny little facts."

Rick snorted derisively.

Primo glowered at him. "I do not want sticky fingers on the memories of my friend, so I keep his diary away from the fingers. Now it stays clean."

Gwen smiled nostalgically at Primo. "I remember the fantastic yarns Derek was always spinning about the life he led. No one could tell stories the way he could."

"No one," Primo agreed.

Rick said, "The story about the diamond mines in Brazil is the best one old Derek wrote. If you ask me, he had a stash of sparklers squirreled away somewhere."

Tomasina thought, *Diamonds! That's what Rick was searching for.* The doorbell chimed and she jumped. Brogue, thank God.

Gwen went and led him in. Tomasina introduced him to Primo and Stella first. She noticed Brogue didn't change his neutral expression at any time, although a small muscle ticked in his jaw when she came to Rick.

"You're the big badge on the TV news," Rick said with instant recognition. "The drive-by shooter thing."

Brogue curtly acknowledged, "I got twenty seconds of airtime."

"Well, I gotta go to the john all of a sudden," Rick drawled, standing up. "Cops scare the crap outta me."

"Upstairs," Tomasina said.

Rick followed her directions and went up, trailing the smoke from his cigarette behind him.

When he was gone, Stella made excuses for him. "Ricky tries to be good after leaving a bad life. He improves a little bit."

Primo looked ready to either choke or take a nitro pill.

Tomasina caught Brogue's eye. "I have something to show you in the kitchen, Brogue."

They excused themselves and left the living room. Once in the kitchen, Brogue punched the fist of one hand into the palm of the other.

"If I could nail him with something—anything—I'd lock cuffs on him," he said in an undertone, seething. "Ten to one he's flushing a pocket stash of drugs down the drain right now because I showed up. No thanks to the news spot for putting him on to who I am."

In a hushed voice, Tomasina repeated Rick's statements about the diary and diamonds.

Brogue cursed, then, seeing her tense expression, calmed himself. "How are you doing, anyway?"

Her tone relaxed. "Much better."

"I'm glad. Your mom is great."

"She doesn't think too badly of you, either," Tomasina replied. "She's no happier than I am about Kat's garden, however."

Brogue winced. "Don't get *her* on my case, too." He glanced at the rows of jars. "Any more miracles?"

"The miracle will be if you change your mind about butterfly habitats, Brogue."

"Look, I go get your mom at the airport, I work murders all day and through dinner, and now I get hassled by my main squeeze. Don't I even get a kiss for my trouble?"

Tomasina gave him a big one and he made the most of it, leaving them both breathless when it was over.

"By the time your mom leaves, I'm going to be so hard up for you," he murmured, holding her tight.

"You're not the only one, Brogue."

"You could call me around midnight and we could share a fantasy over the phone," he suggested in a low, wicked tone.

She pretended to be shocked. "With my mother in the next room? Anyway, I'm sure it's against the law, isn't it?"

He shook his head slowly. "Just call me. Let's keep in touch any way we can."

"I need my sleep, bad boy." She paused. "But if your phone rings at midnight tonight . . ."

"I'll wait up for your call," he promised.

She felt her cheeks tint. "I've never done such a thing."

"Neither have I." He looked slightly abashed, himself. "We'll both be virgins."

"Not tonight," she decided. "Some other time."

They could hear Gwen in the living room calling to them, "Tomasina, Brogue, we're missing you."

Brogue muttered back, "Tomasina and Brogue are missing each other."

They left the kitchen to rejoin the others, and found Primo and Stella getting up to leave. Rick was coming down the stairs. Everyone moved to the front door.

Tomasina thanked them for the flowers they'd brought, and for paying a visit. After a flurry of hugs and *ciao*s, they were on their way, with Rick slacking behind.

Brogue left a few minutes later to get back to work.

"Poor Primo and Stella," Gwen said afterward as she gathered up the coffee cups and cake plates. "How do they stand her nephew?"

Tomasina opened a window to air out the room. "It's all in the *famiglia*, Mom. The tie that binds."

"Primo isn't looking well," Gwen mused.

Tomasina rolled her eyes. "Angina plus Rick would be a strain on anyone." She told Gwen about Rick's thievery from the magic shop, but remained silent about him being the assailant next door.

"Megadeth," Gwen said, quoting the word on Rick's T-shirt with a shiver.

"A heavy-metal rock group, Mom, in case you didn't know."

"Even worse is all that piercing of his nose and ears," Gwen said with another shudder. "Poor Primo and Stella," she repeated.

Tomasina's aversion to Rick was much stronger. Stronger than she would ever let Gwen know, unless the evidence against Rick somehow became more than circumstantial. She prayed for a break in the case—she didn't know how much longer she could stand seeing him free as a bird. Free to walk right into her own home!

"REMINDING GWEN of my words to her wasn't as productive as I'd hoped," Samantha fussed to Derek and Kat. "You saw the effect they had on Tomasina—in one ear and out the other."

"Your words may yet take hold in her philosophy of life," Kat said hopefully. "Prompt Gwen to repeat them two more times. You always said your students needed to hear something three times before they'd remember what you told them."

Derek was impatient with so much talk about emotions. "We have more serious problems than mere love to resolve, ladies. A criminal has to be brought to justice for his attack on Tomasina."

"We failed to prevent it," Sam said, stewing. "She froze and couldn't move, no matter how hard we pushed at her."

Kat said, "I don't understand how she got the feeling that something was wrong that night. We certainly didn't wake her—we wouldn't put her in that kind of danger. What did it?"

"Bad vibes," Derek answered. "My diamonds will end up in criminal hands if my mission doesn't succeed. None of our three efforts has paid off yet. We've got to take action, but hell if I know just what action to take this time."

They all looked at one another, stumped for an answer.

"I've got it!" Kat exclaimed with sudden inspiration. "We've been overlooking some of the most natural wonders in the world."

Sam and Derek perked up. "What wonders?"

When Kat told them her plan, there were big smiles all around again.

TOMASINA AWOKE the next morning and heard her mother making breakfast downstairs. She could smell coffee and bacon.

Three minutes later she padded to the kitchen in slippers and her bathrobe. "Mmm, coffee. Mmm, bacon. Mmm, waffles," she murmured, hugging Gwen good-morning.

"Sit," Gwen ordered. "I'm going to baby you. How do you feel today?"

Tomasina sat down at the table. She curved her hands around the cup of steaming coffee Gwen set in front of her.

"I'm definitely on the mend, Mom. Today I'm starving."

"I've got just what you need for that," said Gwen, popping two frozen waffles into the toaster.

After a sip of coffee, Tomasina told her, "I had the most vivid, amazing, realistic dream last night. About Derek."

"You're in love with Brogue, but dreaming about Derek?"

"Mom, Derek showed me his diary in the dream and told me there were clues in it about where he hid a metal box full of diamonds. Worth millions, he said."

"After last night's conversation, it's not surprising that you'd dream about it," Gwen reasoned. "In fact, I had a dream about Sam, who was mentioned last night, too."

"What happened in yours?"

"Sam appeared, saying over and over, 'True love is worth any cost.' As if I haven't already learned that."

"I can't understand how you believe it, Mom."

"Tomasina, do you think I'd rather not have had Reece and Keely and you to love, even if I eventually lost all *three* of you to similar tragedies? What would have been the good of living without loving?"

Tomasina said, "Some odds are higher than others."

"Some loves," Gwen countered, "are greater than others. Worth any cost. When Brogue asks you to marry him, remember Sam's words."

"Brogue and I aren't talking marriage."

Gwen gave her a faraway smile. "I have a fond memory of saying the same thing about myself and Reece.

Two weeks later, I ate my words. Nine months after that, Keely was born."

They were both silent for several long moments, cherishing their memories.

Brushing a tear away, Gwen smiled again. "I have my hopes up for you and Brogue whether you like it or not."

TOMASINA COULDN'T get the dream of Derek out of her mind, even after Gwen went back to L.A. two days later.

It haunted her enough that she told Brogue about it the first night they had together after Gwen's departure.

"If you ask me, dreams don't mean much," Brogue said. "Except the ones I've had about you, I mean."

He went on to describe the yellow, see-through minidress dream. "You called me your wild Irish Brogue," he said. And since she was in bed with him when he related that dream, it wasn't long before they were enacting it together in rapturous, ecstatic detail.

The next morning, Brogue got several promising new leads on the drive-by shootings and had to lose himself in pursuing them. Still haunted by the dream about Derek, Tomasina did some shopping downtown. On a sudden impulse, she hopped a cable car to North Beach and dropped into the magic shop.

Rick was there, ignoring two browsing customers when she walked in, but Primo was out.

"Unc's at the racetrack," Rick said. "What are you up to?"

Deciding to rattle Rick's cage, Tomasina replied, "I thought I might borrow Derek's diary from Primo. It sounded so interesting, especially the part you mentioned about the diamonds."

Rick shrugged, looking unrattled. "I haven't seen it since a few days after you had lunch with Unc. Like he said the other night, he keeps it out of my sticky fingers."

Rick emphasized his words by waggling his nicotine-stained fingers at her in a particularly unsavory way. She was thankful that she wasn't alone with him in the shop. The two customers weren't paying any attention, but their presence made her feel safer than she would have felt otherwise.

"Are you and that cop a hot item?" Rick asked.

She replied, "He has an option to buy the house next door."

Rick raised an eyebrow. "Nobody knows who vandalized it, huh?"

Tomasina looked him in the eye. "The vandal knows, and also knows what he did to me."

"You bet he does," Rick agreed, his eyebrow rising higher. "Desperate people do desperate things when they're up against a wall."

Sick of him and his double-talk, she moved to the door. "Ask Primo to call me when he gets back."

She went home and Primo phoned later in the afternoon.

"The diary is gone from the safe place in my office," he lamented. "Also is fifty dollars gone from there. *Basta*, Rick! Enough!"

Tomasina sympathized with him about his family difficulties. She cheered him up with a little joke, then told him she'd just wanted to read the diary for old times' sake.

"Not to look for Derek's whopper diamonds, eh, *cara?*" he teased, sounding less upset.

"Not in the least. But I've been curious whether he wrote anything in the diary about a tunnel between Kat's house and mine. I recently found one connecting both basements and I'm not sure why it's there. Would you happen to know?"

"Let me think," Primo said. There was a pause. "Maybe Derek make a tunnel to visit a lady love he cannot marry."

"Of course. That's it! I should have guessed it myself." How obvious it seemed now. The tunnel had preserved Aunt Sam's maidenly reputation by allowing Derek to visit her without his being seen going in and out of her house. "You knew about him and Aunt Sam, then."

"*Sì.* A great love was theirs."

"Primo, again you're a genius."

He sighed. "Not so genius. I cannot make Rick go poof!"

"Primo—"

"*Cara,*" he cut in. "I hear a customer come into the shop. I must go. *Ciao.*"

His line clicked off and Tomasina heard a quick click follow it before the dial tone sounded. *Rick*, she thought, *listening on the shop extension.*

After talking to Primo, Tomasina began to wonder if a metal box might, just might, be buried in that very secret tunnel.

There was an easy way to find out, too. She phoned an equipment rental company, rented a metal detector and a hard-hat equipped with a headlight, and arranged for them to be delivered that afternoon.

The delivery came late, just before she left to meet Brogue at a café near his office for a quick dinner. Once at the restaurant, she told him about her impulsive visit to the magic shop and related what Rick had said.

She summed up, "Then Primo called later and said Rick stole the diary and fifty dollars. Rick swears to Primo he doesn't know where it is, of course. Or where the missing money is, either."

Brogue said disgustedly, "Lies upon lies. Solari's a miserable lowlife. Primo should boot him back to Brooklyn, family or not."

Tomasina sighed. "Now I wish I'd never said anything about the diary. That dream just won't leave my mind, though—Derek, the metal box, the tunnel between my house and—" She broke off and gulped, realizing what she'd inadvertently blurted out.

"Tunnel?" Brogue questioned, looking mystified. "Between your house and what?"

"Um, it's something I haven't mentioned before. The right time never came up to tell you, and . . . well . . ." She took a deep breath. "There's a secret underground tunnel connecting my house and Kat's."

Brogue was staring at her, his eyes sharpening with suspicion and distrust. "'A secret underground tunnel,'" he repeated evenly.

Tomasina sheepishly revealed how Airwick had accidentally found the lever in the basement. She explained what purpose she thought the tunnel had served for Derek and Samantha. Finally, she came entirely clean and confessed that she'd used the tunnel to howl in the basement that one night.

Brogue, she could see when she'd finished, was not amused to know she'd been withholding something from him. However, he looked intrigued about the tunnel.

"Come home with me and I'll show it to you," she invited. "Half of it will be yours if escrow closes on the house after you buy it."

"Can't," he replied. "Got to get back to work. The drive-by case is ready to break any minute." He gave her a narrow look. "What do you mean *if* escrow closes?"

She replied, "The tunnel is undoubtedly an illegally built passageway that doesn't comply with any building codes. It could hold up the sale of the house, or block it, if the title company is notified about it."

"It's half on your property," he reminded her, "and could mean a big expenditure in code-compliance repairs for you. If you've been keeping this to yourself hoping to block my buy with the information—"

"No, Brogue," she interrupted. "That wasn't my intention. If we both keep the tunnel a secret, nobody else will ever know. However, now that you've mentioned what preventing the sale could mean for the garden, I can't just ignore it."

He said, "You're thinking you can use it against me, aren't you? The deal would be that you won't reveal the tunnel, and I'll promise to keep the garden as it is."

"It would be for a good cause," she said hopefully.

"No deal, Tomasina. I don't want a few ridiculous insects to come between us, but apparently you do. You've manipulated me, you've deceived me, you've withheld the facts from me."

"And you," she accused in return, "have kept your mind and heart closed about the garden."

Brogue threw down his napkin. "I've just about had it with you and your bugs."

"Good, because I've had it with you and your hard heart!" She threw down her own napkin and snatched up her purse. "We were all wrong for each other in the first place and this just proves it!"

Heads were turning in the café, but Tomasina was too incensed to care.

"'Wrong' is the understatement of the year!" he retorted. "You're a damned impossible dreamer!"

"And you're the cynic of the century!" she flung back, at the same time plunking enough cash on the table for her half of the dinner check.

"Better to be a cynic than chase butterflies and rainbows!"

"Better to chase *them* than waste time with a burned-out cop!"

She got up, stormed out of the café, caught a taxi on the street corner and cried all the way home.

13

ATHOME, Tomasina dried her tears. Sobbing her heart out about Brogue would get her nowhere. She vowed to carry on as if she had never loved him.

To keep herself busy and push him out of her mind, she decided to hunt for buried treasure in the tunnel. For company, she went out to the garden and called Airwick.

He came running into the beam of light from her hard-hat lamp and trotted home with her. She took him, the metal detector and a shovel down to her basement.

He chirred with excitement when she opened the door to the tunnel. Darting in as he'd done before, he went sniffing to the other end, where he scratched on the other door. Tomasina unlatched it and set it ajar to help her feel less closed in.

She turned on the metal detector, adjusted the power and tested it on the shovel. The machine beeped, as it was supposed to whenever it sensed metal.

She began her search at the farther end of the tunnel, backing up slowly toward her own basement. Whistling while she worked—because she still disliked the creepy, gravellike atmosphere—she swept the metal detector in gradual, side-to-side arcs over the earthen floor. Not very far from Kat's door, the machine beeped.

Tomasina dug in that spot and turned up a rusty iron spike. Airwick sniffed it curiously.

"Not quite buried treasure, is it?" she said.

She took up the detector again and continued. Right, left, back and forth. It was a lot like using a weed trimmer. The motion was repetitive, hypnotic, allowing her mind to drift. It drifted to thoughts of Brogue, unfortunately.

She wondered where he was, what he was doing, whether he was in as much turmoil as she was . . .

BROGUE'S OFFICE PHONE was ringing and he was ticked off at it. He was ticked off at everything, except for the knowledge that the drive-by case had just broken.

The derelict who had witnessed the bus-stop shooting had completed detox treatment since then. He'd undergone hypnosis earlier today to remember the scene. His recall of a license-plate number led to a suspect, who had made a full confession ten minutes ago.

Brogue swore at the phone and picked it up. "Homicide. Donovan."

The caller, to his total surprise, was Rick Solari.

"I got a confession to make," Rick said. "About some vandalism and an assault."

Brogue grabbed a pen and paper to take notes. "So tell me all about it, Rick. Get it off your chest."

Rick started talking and within two minutes what he said put Brogue's hair on end.

THINKING ABOUT Brogue brought tears to Tomasina's eyes. She talked to Airwick to stop the thoughts while she swept the metal detector back and forth. Suddenly, in the middle of the tunnel, the detector beeped.

"Here we go again, Airwick. What've we got this time? Hey, this is where you dug a little hole the first day."

Taking up the shovel, she started to dig. Two feet deep she hit something. Something more than an iron spike. Dirt turned right and left from her shovel as she exposed what the detector had found. It took some time to uncover the top completely and dig all around it, as well.

"Airwick, look! Something boxlike." A six-inch oblong, it was wrapped in heavy, deteriorating plastic.

Excited by her find, she lifted it to ground level, tore away the stiff covering, and discovered a metal box like the one in her dream. The hasp on the box was corroded, but the rest of the container was rust-free. She used the shovel blade to pry the hasp loose.

Then she whispered, "Open Sesame," and lifted the lid. Inside was a leather pouch. She had a childhood memory of Derek smoking a pipe and filling the pipe with fragrant tobacco from a leather pouch just like this.

It was Derek's box, no doubt about it. She took out the pouch and poured the contents into the palm of her hand.

Diamonds! Glittering, sparkling, dazzling gems!

"Oh, my God," she breathed.

Suddenly a bright light came in on her from the door to Kat's basement. Startled, she looked up. The light advanced toward her. She tried to shade her eyes, but was too blinded to see who was shining it at her. She tried to think of who knew about the tunnel.

"B-Brogue?" she stammered. "Brogue? If that's you, you're frightening me."

"The diamonds," a voice said, "are mine."

She recognized the voice and was stunned. Too stunned to speak or think for a paralyzed moment.

"Mine," it repeated.

"No," she countered, the word shaking as it left her lips.

"Give them to me."

"No. Derek led me to them in my dream. He wants *me* to have them, not you."

Still blinded by the light, she closed her hand around them and started backing toward the door to her basement.

"Stop! I have a gun to stop you."

"W-why are you doing this? What do you want?"

"The treasure and your silence."

In the beam of the light, Tomasina saw a gun point at her.

She tossed the diamonds to the ground. "Take them, then. You don't need to shoot me."

"I must silence you."

The air seemed to explode with sound. The force of it slammed her backward to the ground. An agony of pain gouged into the left side of her chest and overcame her. She realized she'd been shot. The bright light grew dim.

Staring up, moaning, she vaguely saw Primo step over her and close the door to her basement. He came back and gathered up the diamonds, dropping them into the metal box. *Plink, plink.* One after another. Then the sounds stopped. Primo stood over her, pointing the gun at her.

Through a gray fog of pain, she heard him say, "*Addio, cara.* I beg you, forgive me for this."

She heard the faint click of him readying a shot. She tried to beg, to plead for her life, but she could not move or speak. Her eyes closed. *This is the end*, she thought as she slipped farther and farther from sound and pain. *Brogue!* her mind called out. *I love you!*

"Dead," she heard Primo mumble. She knew he meant her.

DRIVING HIS PORSCHE at top speed, followed a mile behind by two patrol cars, Brogue reached Tomasina's house with a squeal of tires and a scream of brakes.

Busting out of the Porsche, he hit the ground running. Vaulting up the front steps of the house, he didn't bother to knock on the door. Instead he rammed his shoulder against it and broke it wide open.

He yelled Tomasina's name and got no answer. He'd gotten no answer fifteen minutes ago when he'd phoned her to warn her about the confession Rick had made. Brogue sincerely hoped she was out somewhere with friends or even on a date. Either way, she'd be safe. He was taking no chances with her safety, though, not after Rick's call.

Rick had confessed to being at the scene of both crimes—the first vandalism and the second one when Tomasina had been knocked unconscious.

Brogue shouted her name again and started going through the house, upstairs first, then downstairs. No Tomasina. Rushing down the stairs, he found Airwick at the bottom, looking up at him.

"What the hell are you doing inside?"

The skunk darted toward the kitchen, then turned facing him and made a churring sound. Brogue headed into the living room. The skunk darted in his path and blocked it.

"What's your problem?"

Airwick went toward the kitchen again, turned again and churred. Brogue was ready to yank the animal aside, when his sixth sense told him Airwick could be trying to tell him something. Tomasina had said Airwick was as smart as any dog or cat—maybe smarter.

He was definitely acting like Lassie right now, directing a rescuer to a rescue.

"Okay, okay. I'll go that way. It better not just be to your food bowl."

Airwick scampered ahead into the kitchen and then to the door leading down to the basement. He scratched on the door. Brogue opened it and saw that the basement light was on, but Tomasina wasn't there.

He looked at Airwick. "So?"

Airwick went to the closet under the stairs. Brogue saw that the shelves of one wall were bare. He remembered Tomasina's telling him about the tunnel and how it connected the two houses through the closets. What had she said about Airwick accidentally finding a crack in the corner?

Brogue was kneeling to look for it, when a gunshot went off up above. *Outside, not inside,* Brogue determined from the sound. *Backyard.* He rushed up the stairs faster than Airwick could keep up with him, got Tomasina's flashlight from the kitchen and raced out the back door. Finding nothing in her tiny backyard, he sped to the garden gate.

Rushing through it, he heard a groan. The flashlight picked up a body on the ground. The body moved.

Brogue closed in with the light and recognized Primo. The magician was clutching his chest, moaning, "Heart."

Brogue knocked aside the gun that lay near Primo, put an arm under his shoulders and demanded, "Where's Tomasina?"

"*Cara* dies." Tears streamed down Primo's face as he labored for breath. "I die, too."

He started moaning, or praying, in Italian and Brogue shouted for the patrol cops to come.

"You shot yourself, Primo?"

"No—I fall—the gun shoots off—I think I have heart attack."

"You listen to me, Primo. You don't get to die until you tell me where she is. Where, dammit?"

Primo choked. "Tunnel. Dead."

Brogue refused to register that last word. One of the patrol cops came running from the front.

"Take care of him." Brogue told the officer. "Heart attack and possible bullet wound. Bag the gun."

Another cop arrived and Brogue told her, "Get ambulance aid. Two, just in case."

Brogue ran back to Tomasina's basement. Airwick was there, pawing at a crack near the closet floor. Brogue set him aside, fished a finger into the space and found the lever. It gave way and a wall of shelves swung open.

He saw Tomasina on the floor of the tunnel. Still. Silent. Bleeding.

TOMASINA SWAM UP through a thick, heavy fog toward a faint light and a faraway sound of a familiar voice. The fog pressed against her chest, yet slowly she made progress, up, up to the light, the voice.

Ah, she could hear it more clearly. A broken voice, desperate and hoarse. It prayed, repeated her name, told her, "I love you. I need you. Come back."

She struggled up, closer and closer.

The voice lowered to a pleading whisper. It promised, "I'll never touch one weed in the garden if only you'll live. I'll help you breed millions of butterflies if only you'll live. Whatever it takes, I'll do it, I promise."

She surfaced, her eyes fluttered open and slowly focused on a face, a man, the truest blue knight. It was a painful effort to reply, but she did. She had to respond.

"I . . . heard that . . . Lieutenant."

He stared into her face. "Tomasina?"

"I . . . heard."

"Oh, God, beautiful. I mean every word you heard. I love you and I'm never going to stop."

"I love you, too," she murmured, coming more into focus, realizing she was in a hospital. "I didn't die."

"No, but it's been touch and go. The bullet missed your heart and nicked your left lung. But you're all stitched up now."

Tomasina tried to take a deep breath, but couldn't. "He shot me. Primo."

"Yeah." Brogue clasped her hand and kissed it. "I know. He didn't get away with it. I'll tell you all about it later."

"Tell me now. I'm awake."

"Okay. You came out of surgery a little while ago. Primo had a heart attack—didn't make it."

"Primo," she repeated sadly. "Why Primo?"

"Gambling debts. The heat was on him to pay up. He was desperate, hit the end of his rope. Rick wasn't stealing the shop's profits. Primo was gambling them away at the racetrack."

"Rick. Did he hit me on the head or did Primo?"

"Primo. Rick's not a totally bad kid after all. He knew Primo was adding up clues from the diary. Rick spied on him, watched him search in the house, watched him knock you unconscious. He wanted in on the loot if Primo happened to find it. But when Primo bought a gun, Rick got conservative and called me. He didn't want to witness a murder—or Primo's suicide."

"Who found me?"

Brogue smiled. "I did. With a lot of help from Airwick."

"Thank you." Tomasina sighed. "This is all so ironic. Me being shot, I mean."

Brogue agreed, "It sure is. You wouldn't get close to me because you were afraid I'd get killed, yet you ended up with a nearly fatal wound."

"I see now that we're all vulnerable, cops or not," she murmured. "Just being alive is full of risks."

He nodded. "I wish you could have learned that some other way."

"It won't ever come between us again, Brogue." She shared a loving gaze with him, then asked, "What else happened that I don't know about?"

"Something big. The diamonds are all yours, since they were buried in your half of the tunnel. I got an eyeball appraisal on them and you're worth about three million dollars now."

She blinked. "I'm rich?"

"Now you probably won't marry me," he said a little ruefully. "All I can afford is this." He took an engagement ring set with a small diamond out of his pocket.

"Oh, Brogue. I love it."

"You've taught me to hope again, Tomasina. Give me and my bullet scars a chance with you."

"I can live with yours," she lovingly replied, "if you can live with mine."

HOVERING IN a discreet corner of Tomasina's hospital room, the three ghosts congratulated themselves and one another for successfully accomplishing their missions.

"Three million dollars," said Kat, "will enable Tomasina to donate my house and garden to the Flying Flowers Society."

Derek nodded with hearty satisfaction. "My diamonds are finally benefiting someone."

"How romantic," said Samantha with a sigh. "With nothing left to worry about, what a lovely wedding we'll attend."

BROGUE SLIPPED the engagement ring on Tomasina's finger and kissed her lips.

"Forever," he promised.

"Forevermore," Tomasina promised him in return. "As Aunt Sam always said, 'True love is worth any cost,' and now I know why."

This month's
irresistible novels from

Temptation

WHAT MIGHT HAVE BEEN by Glenda Sanders

Lost Loves mini-series

One night of passion had cost Richard Benson dearly. He had
got a girl pregnant and had dutifully married her—but it was
another girl, Barbara Wilson, he loved. Now, single and with a
daughter in tow, Richard was back in town, hoping to recapture
what might have been.

SCANDALS by JoAnn Ross

Grief-stricken over the death of his brother, cynical, hard-
nosed Bram Fortune did the unthinkable—he sought comfort in
the arms of his brother's fiancée. They parted the next
morning, and then Dani came back to him—she was pregnant
with *his* child.

TROUBLE IN PARADISE by Lisa Harris

Archer Smith was looking for peace, but this was shot to
ribbons when he saw his neighbour, sexy Rita O'Casey. He
wasn't the only man watching her, and there was trouble
brewing.

A TRUE BLUE KNIGHT by Roseanne Williams

Tomasina Walden avoided cops so, when she heard that
Detective Brogue Donovan was planning to move in next door,
she told him the house was haunted. Rather than scare him off,
her ghost story seemed to bring out his protective instincts…

Spoil yourself next month
with these four novels from

Temptation

GOLD AND GLITTER by Gina Wilkins

Lost Loves mini-series

When Michael Spencer came to work for Libby Carter, she
tried to quell her unwanted attraction to his rugged, sexy looks.
He had obviously been hurt badly in the past and he was a man
who was used to moving on…

LADY OF THE NIGHT by Kate Hoffmann

Annabeth Dupree wasn't a call girl although it was true that
she had inherited a bordello! How could she convince
everyone—including Zach Tanner—that she wasn't the bad
girl they thought? Especially when the look in Zach's eyes told
her he was starting to *like* this bad girl…

MOLLY AND THE PHANTOM by Lynn Michaels

The princess and the jewel thief. Two greater opposites
couldn't be found, except that Princess Molly needed the
dashing, devil-may-care Chase Sanquist's help. He intended to
steal the Phantom, the centrepiece of her crown jewels—and
she wanted him to do exactly that.

THE BOUNTY HUNTER by Vicki Lewis Thompson

Tough and independent, Gabe Escalante was a man of justice
and was closing in on a dangerous criminal. Dallas Wade was
the next intended victim and suddenly Gabe wanted to be more
than her bodyguard. It could prove to be a fatal mistake.

Temptation

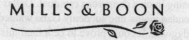

Lost Loves

'Right Man...Wrong time'

All women are haunted by a lost love—a disastrous first romance, a brief affair, a marriage that failed.

A second chance with him...could change everything.

Lost Loves, a powerful, sizzling mini-series from Temptation continues in June 1995 with...

Gold and Glitter
by Gina Wilkins

MILLS & BOON

GET 4 BOOKS AND A MYSTERY GIFT

Return this coupon and we'll send you 4 Temptations and a mystery gift absolutely FREE! We'll even pay the postage and packing for you.

We're making you this offer to introduce you to the benefits of Reader Service: FREE home delivery of brand-new Temptations, at least a month before they are available in the shops, FREE gifts and a monthly Newsletter packed with information.

Accepting these FREE books and gift places you under no obligation to buy, you may cancel at any time, even after receiving just your free shipment. Simply complete the coupon below and send it to:

HARLEQUIN MILLS & BOON, FREEPOST, PO BOX 70, CROYDON, CR9 9EL.

No stamp needed

Yes, please send me 4 free Temptations and a mystery gift. I understand that unless you hear from me, I will receive 4 superb new titles every month for just £1.99* each postage and packing free. I am under no obligation to purchase any books and I may cancel or suspend my subscription at any time, but the free books and gifts will be mine to keep in any case. (I am over 18 years of age)

1EP5T

Ms/Mrs/Miss/Mr _____

Address _____

_____

_____ Postcode _____

mps MAILING PREFERENCE SERVICE